Bend or Break

By

Aaron Waxman

Copyright © 2024 Aaron Waxman

All rights reserved.

No part of this publication may be reproduced, distributed, or transmitted in any form or by any means, including photocopying, recording, or other electronic or mechanical methods, without the prior written permission of the publisher, except in the case of brief quotations embodied in reviews and certain other non-commercial uses permitted by copyright law.

Chapter One

William loosened his necktie as he walked across the green grass of the manicured park field. The gentle rustle of leaves overhead played a harmonious melody with his footsteps, creating a soundtrack to accompany his determined stride.

The maroon stripe of the tie matched his private school uniform blazer perfectly. His senses embraced the natural symphony around him—the distant chirping of birds, the soothing rustle of the breeze through leaves, and the distant hum of the city. The park, a sanctuary of serenity, cradled him in its tranquil embrace. He carried a leather bag that was more like a briefcase than a backpack, having decided at fifteen years old that he was far too mature and fashionable for the latter. He was smiling as he crossed the field from north to south, and at least twice, he ran his finger through his clean-cut, if not a little long, dark hair. School was out, not just for the day but for the whole week of spring break, and this meant the afternoon ritual of walking the three-quarters of a mile from Woolstead Academy.

Woolstead was the premier private school (prep school was the polite term these days) in southern New Hampshire, and William fit the mold. Starting with his parents, his father was in finance, and his mother was active in the community. Finance was code for works on Wall Street, although not *on* Wall Street. Active in the community was code for stay-at-home mothers with children too old to tend to constantly. The Blakes lived in the right house, in the right neighborhood. They didn't keep up with the Joneses; in this community, they were the Joneses. Their residence stood as a beacon of affluence, with manicured lawns and elegant architecture. The envy of neighbors lingered like a silent tribute to the Blakes' unrivaled status, creating an atmosphere where opulence and influence seamlessly intertwined.

William continued his daily walk across the park. It wasn't a leisurely stroll as much as a march toward a destination. A park bench, in this case. As he approached the bench where he spent his afterschool time, he saw his best friend Eddie crossing from the south end to meet him.

Bend or Break

Eddie and William had been inseparable since they met in second grade when Eddie's family moved into the house two streets away. William was Eddie's friend in school when he didn't have any. From an early age, they found socializing with each other somehow easier and more natural than interacting with the other students. Their bond, forged in the crucible of childhood innocence, weathered the storms of adolescence. Shared secrets, laughter, and adventures stitched the fabric of their friendship, a tapestry woven with threads of loyalty that only strengthened as the years unfolded.

Fast forward eight years, and not much had changed besides the boys' heights. Eddie now attended the public school only a mile from Woolstead, so while the boys couldn't interact during the day, it was easy enough to meet one another when the final bells rang, and students from both schools poured out the doors to continue their day in study or sport or socializing or video games.

Eddie wore sneakers and jeans and a light blue T-shirt, not the uniform of Woolstead, but the outfit of choice at Grissom High School (The small town of Galvin had one public high school and two private *prep* schools). He and

William were similarly built, lean but healthy, but Eddie's hair was a messy mop of curls that cascaded around his light-complexioned face. His eyes were grey and caught the reflection of the sun on this afternoon.

The park was just about halfway between the two schools but was sparsely used. The running paths were busy mid-morning when stay-at-home moms went jogging after sending their children off to school, but it was almost empty between three and four in the afternoon when William and Eddie would meet. Just as Eddie could see William, and he knew William could see him, he began to flail his arms in the air as if trying to get someone's attention. William smiled, a silent acknowledgment of their unique and unspoken language, a bond deeper than words could convey.

"Here I am!" Eddie shouted, far too loud for the distance between the boys. William's smile widened, and his eyes glinted. Eddie continued the farce until the two reached the bench, where they would forget about the rest of the world. For about an hour, they could forget about exams and family and let the few worries of their teenage lives waft away. The banter always started the same.

"How was school?" William asked, the smile slowly relaxing on his face.

"Same old, same old," Eddie invariably responded.

"You said it. Did you have that chemistry test today?" William was the more studious of the two and made a habit of checking on Eddie's schoolwork. The same question from his mother would have bothered Eddie, but William had a way of inquiring that didn't spark his indignation.

"Yeah. It was okay. I had a cheat sheet." Eddie may have been less studious, but he was certainly cunning and undoubtedly the risk-taker of the pair.

"Well done," William said encouragingly, although he didn't altogether approve of Eddie's methods. "We had to sit through a two-hour assembly about how important it is to do well on our end-of-the-year exams. Like we don't already know. Like we aren't thinking about these things twenty-four-seven anyway."

"Did you sleep through it?" Eddie asked with his devious smirk.

"No," William said flatly, as though the thought never occurred to him. He gave his best friend credit for not participating in anything he didn't fully sanction.

"Oh," Eddie said, as if the notion of *not* sleeping through such an assembly was the absurd idea. "I would have."

"I should have," William said encouragingly, "We're partying late tonight."

"Are we still chilling at your place?" Eddie asked, although he already knew the answer. They had been planning this evening for some time.

Finally, having concluded the opening ceremonies of their afternoon meetup, the two boys commenced the business of the session. Eddie was sitting on the back of the bench with his feet on the seat, his backpack balanced between his shoes. William sat on the seat of the bench with his backpack in his lap. From it, he retrieved a small pencil case. It was red with a delicate drawstring. He opened the pencil case and gently emptied the contents into his hand. First, a small bag fell out, then a glass pipe. The aroma of marijuana was immediate and unmistakable. William handed the marijuana and pipe to Eddie.

"Would you like to do the honors?" he asked as Eddie took the supplies. He returned the pencil case to his school bag as Eddie used his teeth to untie the bag and put a small amount of the dried herb into the pipe's bowl. He looked at William briefly as though to ask for permission to smoke, and the expression on William's face reminded him that their friendship was established well beyond trivial formalities. Eddie rolled up his right pant leg the way a bicyclist would so it didn't catch in the chain, but he was not preparing to ride a bike. He retrieved a lighter from his sock, where it had been tucked away safely all day. It was a red Bic lighter, the same shade as William's pencil case. Eddie lit the Bic, put the pipe to his lips, and introduced the flame to the weed. He drew a deep breath, closed his eyes, and offered the lighter and pipe to William, who eagerly accepted it. As William repeated the act, Eddie exhaled a puff of smoke as his eyes glazed over. When William had his drag, the two boys looked at each other, lost in thought. While it was getting later into the afternoon, and each had accomplished much for the day, both shared the sentiment the day was just getting started, really. When the high had settled in, and the boys regained their wits, Eddie remembered there was more planning to be done.

"Did you get your sister to get us some beer?" he asked.

"Not yet," William began to explain. "My parents aren't leaving until after dinner. She'll drop them off and pick up the beer on the way home from the airport."

"Sounds like a plan. I'll come by after dinner, and we'll see…" but William interrupted Eddie before he could finish.

"Come over for dinner," he suggested. He knew he would have to insist.

"No, that's okay," Eddie started. When they were younger and still lived in the same neighborhood, they were at each other's houses almost every night for dinner. At first, they had to ask their mother's permission before inviting the other over, but it became so common that the moms assumed if someone came over to play, he was staying for dinner. This often turned into a sleepover, which could extend into the following day's dinner as well. The boys had only grown closer over the years, but since Eddie's family moved from the neighborhood, he seemed uneasy about coming over for dinner.

Bend or Break

"Don't be silly. Come see Mom and Dad off, and then we can have an adventure." William cut in. He couldn't remember the last time Eddie had seen his parents and sister.

"Okay," Eddie conceded. "You got me." He shook his head violently as if to wake himself up.

"Yeah," William said. "I'm going to need an energy drink for the night we have ahead. Let's stop by the store and head to my place."

"Let's do it," Eddie agreed. He re-tied the marijuana bag and gave it to William, who returned it to his red pencil case and stowed it in his leather bag. The boys were red-eyed but ready for the next part of the evening. They rose from their bench and progressed slowly to the edge of the park where the convenience store stood, William in his loose-tie uniform and Eddie in his jeans, sneakers, and blue T-shirt. Eddie mumbled the tune to one of their favorite songs as they strode the patchy grass north.

As they entered the convenience store, Eddie nudged William and looked at the clerk. She was tall, with red hair extensions and green press-on fingernails. The boys exchanged amused glances, slightly bewildered by the vibrant character behind the counter as they navigated the aisles in search of snacks. She was giving a vibe that said, "Don't mess with me," down to the ends of her fake eyelashes. Eddie smiled, and William shook his head. He knew what was coming. Eddie saw the opportunity, and he was certainly going to take it.

"Look," he said loudly enough for the clerk to overhear. "You've got a girlfriend. You shouldn't be cheating every weekend." The truth was that neither of the adolescents had ever had girlfriends, but the long-lashed clerk did not know this. William was reluctantly sucked in. He was now a prop in the fictional scene Eddie was creating. He went along.

"I know, I know," he said half-heartedly. "But she practically begs me to do it. She doesn't care."

"With her sister?" This was a new escalation that Eddie must have come up with in the moment because both boys started laughing but quickly regained their composure and continued the farce. William chose an energy drink from the display case housing an endless variety. They started walking toward the cash register. Just enough time for a final infuriating comment.

Bend or Break

"What she doesn't know won't hurt her," William insisted as they approached the woman behind the counter. By now, one of her eyebrows was raised, and she appeared none too pleased. She scanned the can and told William the price with an extra helping of contempt. William tapped his card and waited for the machine to process the payment, all under the disapproving glare of the clerk. As they left, they heard distinctly from behind them, "You're lucky you ain't my boyfriend," and they started laughing uncontrollably. It was innocent enough because it was made up, right? They both supposed so and laughed for half the walk to William's house. As they arrived, the sun was starting to set in the sky, and the clouds seemed to glow and cling to the last shred of light. The warm hues painted on the horizon cast a serene ambiance that mirrored the quiet anticipation building within the boys. As they walked up the driveway, Eddie realized he would soon be in the presence of William's parents.

"I'm still stoned," he told William apprehensively.

"You look fine," William encouraged. "Besides, you're one of the Grissom boys. My parents will expect you to be selling it by now." This made both boys smile.

When Eddie left Woolstead two years earlier, it would have put a rift in most relationships, but Eddie and William only grew closer over the years, regardless of physical distance. They walked the rest of the way up the driveway and entered through the front door. William's mother, Lynn, was just inside the door organizing her luggage.

"Hi William," she began until she saw Eddie, and her face lit up. "Edward," (She called him Edward.) "How are you doing? We haven't seen you since." She trailed off, but Eddie interrupted her anyway, saving her the embarrassment.

"I'm fine, Mrs. Blake," Eddie said. "How are you?"

"Just fine," she answered, "but we are in a hurry. Go wash up for dinner so Leah can take us to the airport."

Without another word, the boys left to wash their hands as instructed. At the dinner table, they were joined by Lynn, Leah, and William's father, James. As he was not one to mince words or avoid topics, James wasted no time with trivialities, diving into meaningful conversation.

"Edward, I was just reading about the scandal at Grissom," he started.

"You'll have to be more specific, Dad," Leah chimed in. Lynn gave her a sharp look to remind her to mind her manners. Once again, Eddie perceived the situation and knew what to say.

"You mean Ms. Daisly," he said, softly diffusing any tension.

"Yes," James confirmed. "How did it go over?"

"Well, from the first day I was there, everyone gossiped behind her back that she was a drunk. I didn't really know her, but I guess it's good they finally busted her," Eddie gave his insight.

"It's a wonder she lasted eight years as principal," James pondered.

"Well, remember how tight the school's budget is," Lynn added. "They were stretched thin enough before they had to enact all the security measures. The wonder is how they can afford a principal with all the money going toward armed guards." She swallowed and glanced at her husband, avoiding Eddie's eyeline.

"And now we have no principal," Eddie pointed out insightfully. No one had considered this missing resource for the students and the ongoing administration of the school.

"Well, if William went there, I would have done something about it," James declared. Lynn and Leah smirked. William and Eddie laughed outright.

"What would you have done?" Lynn playfully asked.

"Never mind," he changed the subject. "Are you sure we're all packed?" Then, directing his attention to the rest of the table, "Your mother has a talent for forgetting minor things, like her passport." They all laughed.

"We're packed," Lynn confirmed with a bit of indignation.

After dinner, everyone congregated in the entranceway. Lynn was nervously checking and double-checking her purse and going over her list.

"Okay. Tickets, passport, cash - including some Euros," she enumerated. James was trying to ease her stress.

"We can get anything we need over there," then, not realizing he was countering his intent, he added, "Except a passport. Don't forget that."

"You're right," she conceded and then turned her attention toward the top of the stairs, "Leah! Ready?" James turned to William and raised a brow.

"William," he began. "Come talk to me for a minute."

He didn't wait for a response; he led the way to his study down the hallway. He entered first and closed the door when William followed him in. He walked to the desk and handed William an unmarked envelope. "Now, there's plenty here to last you three weeks. That's for food and anything else that might come up. Leah is going to drive my car while we're gone. I don't want you driving without her. Remember, you only have a learner's permit, and I can't bail you out of jail from Paris." They both smiled at this. William was trustworthy, but what parent doesn't give the obligatory warning before leaving town with two teenage children at home alone? It was a standard ritual, a mix of caution and parental instinct. They started walking toward the door. "Also, Jeffery Gordon is going to call and check in a few times. I gave him your cell phone number just in case."

"Don't worry, dad," William insisted. His hands were full of cash, and he was getting a little eager for his parents to leave. "We'll be fine." They went back to the front door, where Lynn was rifling through her purse again.

"William, would you please get your sister and tell her we need to leave?" James asked. William went up the stairs and stopped briefly at his room, where Eddie was waiting.

"We're all set," William said. "Leah is about to leave now." Then he continued down the hall to her room.

"I'm coming," she started when she heard him at her door.

"Wait," he said and pulled the envelope of cash from his back pocket. He opened it and pulled out a twenty-dollar bill. He handed her the money and asked for a twelve-pack of something cheap.

"Is that all?" she asked with a judgmental scoff.

"It's just Eddie and me," William explained. Leah rolled her eyes and took the cash. She didn't care if her little brother only had one friend. She was going to throw the party of the year. The siblings returned to their parents at the front door and went through the formal goodbyes.

"Have a safe trip," William said.

"We'll call you as soon as we get to my sister's," his mother said back.

It was a ritual at this point. William was old enough to take care of himself, and his parents had been traveling his whole life, so this was business as usual as far as he was concerned. Leah left with a car full of parents and luggage and would return soon with a car full of beer and high schoolers. William went upstairs to his bedroom where Eddie had been waiting, the excitement of the night settling over them.

The room was somewhat plain for a high school boy's. There were no posters of rock bands or bikini models. There were no model race cars or fitness magazines. There were a few trophies and medals, although William was the first to point out that they were awarded for academic achievement rather than athletic dominance. The shelves held a curated collection of books, a nod to his intellectual pursuits. A neatly organized desk stood in a corner, adorned with a laptop and a stack of notebooks, further attesting to William's commitment to his studies.

Aaron Waxman

He was more of a math olympiad than a football star, which he had no aspirations to become anyhow. His bed was twin-sized and positioned against a wall with the sheets pulled perfectly taught, reflecting an orderliness that mirrored his disciplined approach to both academics and life.

The walls were pale blue, a color he had chosen a decade earlier and never thought of changing. Eddie sat at his desk, where he had been thumbing through some of William's school work to pass the time. They were debate class briefs William had been working on since the beginning of the semester. Eddie had written a few long essays for English and History classes, but this was another level altogether. He was impressed, but as soon as William entered the room, Eddie put the pages down as though he were holding the Declaration of Independence itself. He was half embarrassed to have been reading the work, and the rest of him just wanted to make sure he didn't ruin the pages in the freak accident that was running through his mind. Something along the lines of him dropping the pages out the window, where they get blown through a stump grinder and struck by lightning. He snapped back to reality when William closed the door, debate briefs unharmed. The imagined catastrophe dissolved, leaving only the relieved exchange of glances between friends.

"Oh shoot!" William said, just realizing something. "I forgot to pick up more pot. Let me call Phillip." Eddie gave him a nod, and William pulled his cell phone from his pocket and called a number saved only as a marijuana symbol. It was not very discreet, but teenagers are not known for their discretion, and these were ordinary teens in most regards. Eddie could hear only one side of the conversation.

"Yo, Phil," William began. His voice was different. More casual, but was there also a tinge of trying too hard? Eddie wasn't sure, but he didn't think William needed to impress the likes of Phillip. "What up?" William continued. "No, I was just seeing if you were good." Pause.

"Okay, I'll be there in ten. Later." He hung up the phone and turned to Eddie. "Shall we?"

They estimated they had about two hours to kill before Leah got back with the beer, which would be plenty of time for the two boys to walk to Phillip's house and back. He lived only a few streets away. In fact, Phillip lived in

Eddie's old house. This stirred up feelings of jealousy and confusion for Eddie, but his interactions with Phillip were always brief and always with William. This gave him comfort, although he was sure Phillip simply didn't like him. The lingering tension added an unspoken layer to their encounters, a subtle undercurrent in the dynamics of friendship and time.

The neighborhood was dark now as they walked slowly down the sidewalk. There were street lamps lighting the way and stars farther above. The clouds had cleared, and the moon was beginning to ascend on the horizon above the trees to the north. They walked without speaking past the first few houses before Eddie broke the silence, his voice cutting through the quiet like a gentle revelation.

"Where are we going to go on an adventure tonight?" He asked.

"I don't know," William answered. "You always have the good ideas. It was true that Eddie was usually one to find new spots to explore. This was because he was the risk taker. He would take them places that William would never dare think to go. This night was no different. As they had been anticipating William's parents leaving for some time, Eddie did have something special planned.

"I found a spot down by the golf course," Eddie started. "There's an old playground on the church side. I don't think they use it anymore."

"Excellent," William agreed. "We can have a few beers and then go smoke out there."

"Perfect," Eddie said through a smile of simple contentment. Just then, they turned up the footpath in the front yard of a house with no lights on. There were no lights on inside or out; to any passerby, it would appear no one was home. William would have had the same thought if he hadn't spoken to Phillip moments earlier. They climbed the steps to the front door, and William knocked. For a moment, there was no sound, and Eddie began to wonder if the place was actually empty. It was strange, as it always was, knocking on what used to be his own front door. The echo of familiarity mingled with the anticipation of the new and unknown.

Finally, the pair standing on the outside could hear the metal cover sliding on the peephole on the inside. A chain slid. The door cracked me open. Phillip was standing on the other side. He was taller than Eddie and William, with straight black hair. He wore baggy skateboarding pants and a hemp bracelet. Eddie wondered if he ever skateboarded or if he just liked to play the part and look the look. The enigmatic aura of Phillip added an air of mystery, raising questions that lingered beneath the surface of casual pleasantries.

"Hey guys," Phillip said flatly as he looked from William to Eddie and back again.

"Hey, Phil. What's going on?" Eddie said back too eagerly. Phillip opened the door to let them in and closed it behind them. The three boys took a few steps toward the stairs, and Phillip stopped and turned to Eddie.

"Wait here," Phillip said coldly. Did he say it coldly, or is that just the way Eddie heard it? No, he was pretty sure there was something behind the way he said it. William and Phillip continued up the stairs, and Eddie heard a door close. He hated waiting. He especially hated waiting in what used to be his own house. He hated waiting for William. The familiar surroundings, tinged with memories, intensified his impatience, a silent reminder of the changes that time had etched on the canvas of their shared history. Upstairs in Phillip's room, there were two more teenagers who William did not recognize.

"Sorry, Phillip. I know you aren't Eddie's biggest fan." William said, feeling a slight warmth touch his cheeks. He hoped he wasn't blushing.

"It's cool," Phillip said. "Don't worry about it. How much do you want?"

"Fifty," William said coolly. Phillip went to his desk and fidgeted in one of the drawers for a moment. "I haven't seen you around school lately." William was filling the silence.

"I'm at St. John's now. Didn't you hear?" Phillip asked.

"No. I hadn't heard. Why the move?"

"I think my father is in some business war with the headmaster at Woolstead. The whole family is boycotting now," Phillip explained, then he turned to one of his other friends in the room and added, "Thank goodness for St. John's, my dad says. Otherwise, Grissom would be the only choice, and I wouldn't wish that juvey center on anyone." They all laughed except William.

"Eddie says it's not that bad," he tried to tell them but knew immediately it was a mistake. It was the second time he mentioned Eddie.

"Right. Anyway. Here you go," Phillip said as he handed William a freshly tied bag of marijuana. "Fifty bucks." William handed him the money, and they each pocketed their newly acquired greenery.

"Well, I guess I better go," William said awkwardly. He was very careful not to mention Eddie again, although all he wanted to say was, "Eddie's waiting," and, "I better get back to Eddie." Phillip saw them out from the top of the stairs, not bothering to follow William down or lock the door after he left with Eddie. As they walked down the pathway back to the sidewalk, William cut the silence again.

"So we're all set. Leah should be back with the beer in about an hour and…," but Eddie cut him off mid-sentence.

"Why does he hate me?" He was exasperated. "I've never done anything but be nice to him. He doesn't even know me."

"He doesn't hate you," William tried to reassure, but it didn't work.

"Yes, he does," Eddie insisted.

"Don't let it bother you," William tried a slightly different tactic. "Like you said, he doesn't even know you." This worked a little, and the knotted frown on Eddie's face loosened a bit. As if to have the final word on the matter, Eddie chimed in again, trying to be more serious than he actually was.

"Fine," he said. "But if he didn't sell, we would probably get into a fight." William had to restrain his laugh. The idea of Eddie fighting anyone was comical to him, and he wasn't letting him get away with the last word.

"If he didn't sell, you would never have met." Both boys laughed at the spiraling nonsense.

Chapter Two

Back at William's house, he and Eddie were in his father's lounge. He called it a lounge, but it was really one part library, one part billiard room, and it didn't have an identity of its own. The room exuded an eclectic charm, a nod to either James's multifaceted interests or his short attention span. It was William's favorite room when he was a child, even though he wasn't allowed to touch anything. Now of the age when touching was allowed, he found he didn't have much of a penchant for billiards or an appetite for the dusty Victorian books his father half-heartedly collected. On this night, it was the perfect place to hide out. Leah had returned with three friends and enough beer for the three dozen others who would arrive shortly after she did. She delivered to William the sole twelve-pack he had requested. No change, as expected. They had agreed on which areas of the house were off-limits during her party. No one upstairs, agreed. No one in Dad's office, agreed. No one in the lounge. Even as they were making the rules, Leah knew they didn't apply to William and Eddie. They weren't destructive. They didn't have to worry about Eddie ruining the felt on the pool table or vomiting in their mother's pillowcase. The rest of the guests were animals, as far as they were concerned.

From their hideout in the lounge, William and Eddie could hear the music and raucous on the other side of the door, and they couldn't be less interested in it. They had their beers to sip; they had their adventure planned for later; they had each other. The distractions outside the lounge held no allure compared to the friendship and shared moments within the familiar confines of their sanctuary. Eddie lazily threw a dart toward the dartboard and missed entirely, the dart embedding itself in the wall about six inches off the board toward seven o'clock. He winced and looked at William, who was laughing and finishing his beer.

"Let's pack a few of these up and go explore," William said. Neither of them liked crowds, and even with a door between them and the rest of the party, they weren't quite in their comfort zone. When they opened the door, the party was more out of control than they expected. The house was trashed, the music was pounding, and Leah was nowhere to be seen. William approached the nearest teen, clearly closer to his sister's age. He turned to Eddie and smiled.

"Crazy party," he said to the teen, "Do you even know whose house this is?"

"Naa, man," The partier responded drunkenly. "Do you?" William gave him a disapproving look and pointed toward the door. The drunken partier left the house while Eddie and William laughed.

"Meet me out front," William continued. "I'm going to make sure Leah's okay." Eddie turned right toward the front door, and William turned left toward the kitchen to see if he could find his sister. He found her in the back room in a circle of people playing some sort of drinking game. They were singing and tapping and stomping, but most of all, drinking. The lively atmosphere, fueled by laughter and clinking cups, enveloped the room in a celebratory haze, marking the night with youthful exuberance.

Through the commotion, William managed to get her attention without saying anything. He gave her a thumbs up with a questioning look on his face. She returned the thumbs up with a confident nod. She had this under control. Their silent exchange conveyed a shared understanding, a bond unspoken yet unwavering. William made a quick gesture with his thumb and pinky to say, "I have my cell phone," and he made his way back through the crowd. Eddie was waiting out front, where a few wayward partiers had come. Among them, one was smoking a cigarette and absentmindedly flicking his ashes into William's mother's flower pots. Eddie led the way to his secret spot, the one by the golf course. He didn't mention to William that they had to cut through the private golf club property to get to the abandoned playground. The thrill of secrecy and the promise of undiscovered places fueled their adventure, adding an element of risk to their escapade.

"No one patrols over here at night," Eddie explained with a confident smile as though he had paid off the armed guard who usually stood post here. William was still nervous.

"Are you sure? Is there another way around?" William asked.

"It's over a mile if we loop around the other way. It's just a quick run across the eighth-hole green, and we can cut through the woods. See?" Eddie's confidence was starting to spread to William, but he wasn't fully convinced. "Don't worry. I promise." This was enough. If Eddie was sure, he was sure. Eddie didn't wait for him to make up his mind; he grabbed William's hand and darted across the green, dragging him until they both broke out into a full sprint. They stopped when they got to the wood line and hid behind a tree.

"You okay?" Eddie asked.

"Fine," William replied. His adventurous spirit was awakened. "Where now?" he smiled back.

"Not far, but be careful you don't trip over any roots," Eddie cautioned.

They quickly cut through the small section of woods between the golf club and the church, and just as Eddie had promised, there was an old playground. It looked like it was once used by the church, but there was a new one now on the other side of the property, and this was left to ruin. The rusted equipment and faded paint whispered stories of bygone laughter, a silent acknowledgment of the passage of time. There was a merry-go-round, a see-saw, and a swing set with chains but no swings. The woods blocked the view from anyone looking from the golf course, and the church was surely empty at this time on a Friday. Any remaining worries William had subsided as he looked around. They were alone. The only sound was the wind in the trees. The abandoned playground, with its nostalgic aura, felt like an undiscovered haven, a retreat from the bustling world, where time seemed to stand still in the company of old memories.

"What do you think?" Eddie asked with his arms out, palms up, like he was showing the place off. He didn't know how much the solitude meant to William, who was overwhelmed by how perfect this dilapidated playground was.

"It's better than I pictured," he admitted. Eddie pulled the packed marijuana pipe from his pocket and handed it to William. He took a puff and gave it back to Eddie. "You know, we never named this one," he said of the glass pipe.

"Let's not," Eddie replied. "Seems like every time we name one, it breaks."

"Yeah," William agreed through glassy eyes. "Let's not." Eddie smoked the marijuana and set the pipe down. He looked up at the stars, still clearly visible, but he didn't know the first thing about astronomy. William pulled two beers from his backpack and handed one to Eddie. They counted to three and drank their whole cans. William staggered a bit and held up one finger to say, "I'm going to need a minute." Eddie smiled at him. Whatever queasiness afflicted William had not hit him. At least not yet. He ran toward the old swing set and shouted, "AAAH OOOH," and leaped toward the chain, which he grabbed onto and swung up high, nearly toppling the whole structure. On his swing back, he let go and came back to the ground, landing on his knees. This was a good position to land in because, seconds later, the sickness found him. Too much beer. Too much motion. It was coming back up, and soon. He tried to say, "Oh my god," but it came out more like uh-meh-guh, and the vomit followed. William had just found his balance and was relieved of his vertigo when this happened, so he slowly went to Eddie and rubbed his back.

"I'm okay," Eddie managed to choke out through teary eyes. "It's out. I'm okay."

Bend or Break

"You know, there's a saying in China when someone has a bad idea and still follows through with it," William said with a smirk.

"What?" Eddie struggled.

"You're an idiot." Both boys smiled. "C'mon. Let's get you home," William continued, but they both knew he meant back to William's house. There was no going home in this state for Eddie. On the return trip, the walk through the woods was even slower and more deliberate than on the way in. As they reached the golf course, William walked slowly through the green, looking over his shoulder but with one hand on his friend's back to make sure he didn't stumble. The journey back carried a different rhythm, a pace marked by a shared awareness of both the memories they were leaving behind and the comforting presence of each other.

The next thing they knew, they were both blinking in the sunlight of morning. They were a tangle of limbs, still fully clothed from the night before. William was in his bed, blanket twisted sideways, and Eddie was on a pull-out sleeper bed that normally was rolled tidily out of sight under the main part of William's bed. His light brown hair was a gnarled mess, and there were lines on his face where it had been smashed against the sheet creases. The aftermath of their adventure left its mark, a disheveled nod to the joyous chaos and unfiltered moments that defined their night.

The analog clock on the wall said it was eleven forty-three.

"Hey," William said hoarsely.

"Mmm," was all Eddie could groan.

"How are you feeling," William asked.

"Fantastic."

"What happened last night?"

"I remember drinking at the park, but that's where it goes blurry."

"The park," William marveled. "I completely forgot." He ambled to the mini fridge under his desk and brought back an energy drink for each of them. They both cringed at the sound when they opened the cans but drank heartily.

"Same thing again tonight?" Eddie asked through a slightly pained grin.

"You know it," William half smiled-half grimaced.

"Oh, but we have to call it early tonight," Eddie said. "I have to go home at some point."

"That's right," William remembered. "Big interview tomorrow."

"I'm not worried about impressing a fast-food manager, but I guess it's better not to be hung over," Eddie suggested.

"We'll just have to start early," William began to plan the day.

"I have to make an appearance at home at some point, or my mom won't let me out later."

"Okay. Let's meet for tacos in three hours and get the day going." Eddie gathered his school bag and a few belongings and made his way slowly home.

It was just over two miles, and with his headache, he knew it was going to take a while. William finished his energy drink and made his bed. Within minutes, the room was put back together with no sign of last night's activities. He caught a glance of himself in the mirror and realized he wasn't in such good shape. The reflection mirrored the weariness etched across his features, a subtle reminder of the night's revelry and its toll on his well-being.

After a restorative shower, he found Leah downstairs. She was sitting at the kitchen table, seemingly unaware of the television that was on in front of her or the bowl of cereal sitting before her, which she had prepared and then quickly learned she didn't have the stomach for. The house was trashed, but he knew they had plenty of time to get things in order before their parents returned. The remnants of the night's festivities lingered, but the prospect of personal restoration was prioritized. He poured her a glass of orange juice and set it on the table.

"This might do the trick," he said, but he wasn't sure she could hear him. Thinking he had stumbled onto an opportunity, he pushed his luck. "Can I take Dad's car?" This got her attention, although surprisingly not in a negative way.

"I don't need it 'til eight tonight," she said. "Don't use all the gas, and don't crash. If you get caught, I'm claiming ignorance."

"Deal!" he said through a huge grin. He'd never taken the car on his own, but Leah had dozens of hours with him practicing, and she didn't feel like playing chaperone today. "Drink that juice. You'll feel better."

"Going somewhere with Eddie?" Leah asked with an eyebrow raised.

"Yeah, of course," William responded as though it were a stupid question. Who else would he be spending time with on a Saturday afternoon?

"You two seemed to have fun last night."

William got to the fast-food taco restaurant fifteen minutes early because he wanted it to be a surprise that he had the car. He waited impatiently to see his friend come through the door. There were doors at both ends of the restaurant, so he kept glancing back and forth, tapping his middle finger on the bleach-smelling table where he sat. While he waited, his attention was suddenly torn from the doors when the young woman behind the counter shouted an order number. Her name tag revealed she was Ella. The bustling energy of the establishment permeated the air, a backdrop to the anticipation building within the young man.

A moment later, Eddie walked through the door William was watching, and the two smiled upon seeing each other. Eddie's hair was wet from his shower and combed back. When it dried, it would bob with each step he took and catch in the wind, but now it looked slicked back like a fifties greaser. The thought amused William, whose smile widened. It was a fleeting moment of amusement, a ripple of joy in the midst of ordinary events, underscoring the simple pleasures found in the corners of everyday life. They hugged a quick hello and headed to the counter to order lunch. They both were hungry as it was late in the afternoon, and neither had eaten since before the escapades of the night before. They looked at each other to see who would order first. William stepped forward and was greeted by Ella, the same worker he noticed earlier.

"Would you like to try our new cheesy, crunchy wrapper," she asked enthusiastically. William wondered how many times that day she had asked the same question. How many people had responded 'yes?'

"Not today," he responded, coming back to reality from his thoughts. "Three tacos, please."

"With the works?" Ella asked.

"Yes, please."

"Same for me," Eddie added. They paid Ella a few dollars for their tacos and waited for them ravenously.

"That's going to be you slinging tacos by this time next week," William joked, and both boys laughed at the thought. This is where he was interviewing the next day, and the reality was that he'd be slinging tacos long before this time next week. "So, what's the plan?"

"I don't know," Eddie began, but he always had ideas of what to do on a Saturday afternoon. "We could go to the lake for a while."

"Want to go down to the city instead?" William couldn't contain his smile. He knew this suggestion would give away his secret.

"You have the car?" Eddie was as amazed as he was impressed. William patted his pocket to confirm the keys were in his possession. "Let's go!" Eddie's smile matched William's. They had been to Staunton, what they called The City, many times, but always chaperoned by parents or as tag-alongs with Leah when she got her driver's license. Today was going to be different. They weren't under supervision or on anyone else's schedule.

They devoured their tacos eagerly, and their smiles hadn't faded by the time they made their way to the parking lot to William's father's car. The simple joy of shared moments lingered, a residue of contentment coloring their journey ahead. It was a large sedan, but William had done all his practicing on either this car or his mother's even larger SUV. He was not worried. A short twenty-five-minute drive and they were in downtown Staunton. In truth, it wasn't a big city by most standards, but in terms of southern New Hampshire, it was as big as they come. There was a small business district that the boys drove through to get to their favorite park. Luckily, they found a place to park the car with no trouble (William demonstrating his parallel parking skills). Eddie looked around and breathed the air like a man who had just been released from a twenty-year prison sentence. He felt unrestrained and unjudged, not feelings he was used to. It was nice to be among strangers. The anonymity among the crowd offered a liberating escape, a chance to shed the familiar expectations and immerse himself in the freedom of fleeting connections with those who didn't carry preconceived notions.

They wandered through the park, making note of peculiar-shaped shrubs and stopping to watch a soccer match played by what appeared to be kindergartners. The players' lack of coordination amused William, but some showed talent for their age. William and Eddie walked past the edge of the park and continued to a coffee shop that William remembered from his last visit with his sister. Neither of them really knew the city, so when they got their coffee, they simply wandered the tangle of streets, looking at dogs in fenced yards and joking away the afternoon without a care. The cityscape became a canvas for their unscripted adventure, a maze of discovery and shared laughter.

Suddenly, William felt a buzzing vibration in his pocket. He retrieved his phone and saw Leah was calling. He also saw it was seven forty-five. He answered the call, and again, Eddie could only hear half the conversation.

"Hell-" William began, but Leah must have cut him off because he didn't finish the word. "We're on our way back. We'll be there in ten." He hung up the phone as Eddie checked his watch. There was no way they were going to make it. "Looks like we're taking the interstate back," William smiled nervously. He knew even then they were going to be late, and he wasn't too excited about the idea of driving on the highway. They scrambled to retrace their steps to where they had parked the car and made terrific speed back to the suburbs. The small city's chaos gave way to the familiar calm of the outskirts, a contrast that marked the end of their spontaneous urban escapade and the return to suburban serenity. William would drop Eddie off at his house before getting the car back to his anxiously awaiting sister. As he pulled up to Eddie's house, he wished him luck on his interview in the morning.

"Thanks," Eddie said back. "Let's meet up after. I'll come by your place."

"Sounds good," William confirmed. "Bye."

He rushed back the few miles from Eddie's house to his own. It was only twenty after eight, but he knew his sister would be in a mood. Before he even got to the front door, she was rushing out. She grabbed the keys from him and gave him a look as only an older sister can. The unspoken communication conveyed both concern and authority, a dynamic unique to the bonds of siblinghood.

"I was about to take Mom's car," she exclaimed in her frustration.

"Well, why didn't you?" William replied with a dose of sarcasm that he knew would not help the situation. After all, if he wanted to use the car again while his parents were away, he better stay on her good side. "Sorry," he quickly added. "We lost track of time."

"It's fine," she relaxed her tone. "I'll be back late. Don't wait up." And with that, she was off. William entered the house, closed the door, and relished his time alone. Even if the house was still a mess from Leah's party, he could enjoy a few hours of peace. As though the universe sensed this and sought to delay his calm evening, he felt another buzz in his pocket. The intrusion of the outside world, symbolized by the persistent vibrations, hinted at the unpredictability that often punctuated moments of tranquility. He opened his phone to see he had two voicemail messages. He pressed play and heard his mother's voice.

"William, it's me. We just arrived at my sister's. Everything's fine here. Just checking in. I'll call you again tomorrow." He pressed delete. The next voice he heard was less familiar.

"Hello, William. This is Jeff Gordon. Your father…" He pressed delete, having no interest in hearing the rest of the message. Maybe Jeff was calling about the party. That was Leah's problem to deal with. Maybe he was just checking in. William didn't care.

Chapter Three

The next morning, Eddie found himself sitting at the same taco restaurant he had eaten at with William the previous afternoon. Only this time, he was sitting at a booth across from the store's manager. Eddie wore khaki pants and a polo shirt. The manager was wearing a collared shirt with the taco logo embroidered on the chest. He flipped through the papers to find Eddie's name.

"Well... Eddie. It seems like everything is in order. We're real short right now, so we can definitely bring you on." Eddie was shocked at how easy it was. He wondered if every job interview was so short and simple, and he sincerely doubted it.

"Thank you very much," he said, still thinking the process didn't take much effort.

"How many hours per week can you do?" the manager asked. "Be realistic."

"Maybe twenty or twenty-five," Eddie guessed.

"We'll start with twenty and see how it goes," the manager said. "That actually works out pretty good. Hey... I know we didn't have it planned, but we're about to do an all-staff food safety course this afternoon. If there's any way you could stay, you won't have to sit through it later."

"Yeah," Eddie said, not even thinking about his plans with William. He was still thrilled about his new job and wanted to show he was a team player by staying for the training.

"Great," his new boss said. "They are about to get started. Let's join them."

He led Eddie to the back room. It was strange for Eddie to cross that line from the dining room up front into the back kitchen. The perspective of the whole place changed. The transition between spaces held a transformative quality, revealing hidden corners and the orchestrated chaos of the restaurant's operations. Farther in the back was a small office with too many people crammed around a small computer screen. Most were teenagers like Eddie, working after school. Some were in their twenties, and a few were older. They all looked bored, and one or two looked hung over. Among the teens was Ella, the young woman who had helped him and William the day before and countless other times.

"Okay, everyone. We're about to get started," the manager announced in a raised voice. "This is Eddie. He's starting today." He motioned with his hand for Eddie to join the others. There wasn't much space, but he pushed in near Ella, feeling comfortable with the familiar face, and could mostly see the computer screen through the others crowded around it.

Meanwhile, William was at home. He had woken up early and felt well-rested after he and Eddie took the night off from their usual adventures. He worked on schoolwork for a while but found he was distracted and unmotivated. He began cleaning up some of the mess from his sister's party but also found that didn't hold his attention much. He wasn't worried about Jeff Gordon stopping by to check on them. Even if he knocked at the door, William wasn't inviting him in for a visit. He checked his watch every few minutes, looking forward to meeting up with Eddie as soon as he was done with his interview. After a few hours of doing nothing much at all, Leah appeared downstairs.

"Another late night?" William asked.

"Don't start with me," she warned. "I'm still mad at you for keeping the car late."

"Sorry," he offered. He wanted to use the car again, so it was best to play it safe. He checked his watch. It was eleven fifteen. Eddie would be just starting his interview by William's calculation.

"I'm having a friend over to watch a movie this afternoon," she moved on to a more current topic of conversation.

"A friend?" he asked.

"Danny," she explained.

"Of course," William said with an eye roll, still trying to stay on her good side. He didn't care if she had a guy as long as they left him alone.

"Well, there's one thing," she added, as though she could read his mind. Maybe that was a stretch, but they were closer than they liked to admit, and she knew him pretty well. "Do you know Jennifer Cox in your grade?"

"I think so," he said, but he certainly knew who Jennifer was. She had been in his geometry class the year before.

"Well, that's Danny's little sister, and he said he's stuck with her for the day. I said she could hang out with you and Eddie."

"What?" William asked. He had no desire to add a third wheel to his fun afternoon with Eddie. He knew she wouldn't fit it, wouldn't get their inside jokes. It was going to be like babysitting. "Why did you say that?"

"I'll make you a little deal," she began, and he knew he was going to have to agree to whatever she proposed. It was the nature of their relationship. "You hang out with a girl for one afternoon, and I'll forget you were late with the car last night. You do want to use it again while Mom and Dad are gone, I assume." As usual, she had him right where she wanted him.

"Fine," he acquiesced. It wasn't going to be fun, but it seemed like a fair deal. The siblings spent the next half hour getting the house back in half-decent shape before the madness started again. Yet, as the minutes ticked by, William couldn't shake the looming anticipation of the inevitable socialization.

Leah carried a stack of pizza boxes outside to the barrel trash can while William collected beer cans, the smell of the warm, stale brew turning his stomach. When the place looked almost presentable, there was a buzz in William's pocket. *Finally*, he thought. *Eddie is calling to say he's on his way*. He took his phone out of his pocket and, to his disappointment, it wasn't Eddie. It was Phillip. He answered the call.

"Hello?"

"Hey, man. What's up?"

"Not much. Just about to enjoy some of your lovely offerings," William never knew what to say.

"Awesome. Just wanted to let you know I got something new in. Best stuff I've seen in months. Thought you might want dibs."

"Totally," William said. "I'm busy now, but I'll call you later."

"No prob."

"Save some for me," William asked.

"Will do."

"Alright. Bye."

"Later."

William put his phone back in his pocket and immediately looked at his watch. It was almost one o'clock. *Where was Eddie?* He wondered. Then, another thought occurred to him. This one was much worse. Whatever the reason Eddie was late, he was going to have to entertain Jennifer Cox. He hoped for a moment that she would want to watch the game and hang out with the older kids, but he knew this was a fantasy. Even if she was into sports, which was a real possibility, his sister would find an excuse to get close to Danny, and no one wanted to see her older brother with a girl falling all over him. If it came to it, he would make an excuse to leave. Maybe he needed to go look for Eddie. The possibility of Eddie being in trouble became a plausible reason for his departure, lending urgency to his imaginary quest. He went to the backyard to smoke some marijuana while he waited for whatever was coming. He hoped it was Eddie.

Back at the taco shop, the training video had ended. Ella nudged one of the teens who had fallen asleep in his chair. Eddie noticed and exchanged a quick smile of approval with Ella. The manager entered a moment later with a clipboard.

"Okay. Everyone, please sign the sheet to get credit for the training," he said as he handed the clipboard to Ella. She signed and passed it along. The manager turned to Eddie. "Eddie, are you able to start tomorrow?"

"Sure," he replied, half wanting to be a team player and half thinking of his first paycheck.

"Okay," his boss said approvingly and handed him a slip of paper. "Here's your schedule for the week. One last thing: we've got Mike here today, so it'd be good if you could do a few hours training." Eddie hesitated a moment. He wanted to look at his watch, but he didn't want to seem rude. He felt like he had to agree.

"Sure," he said confidently. "I'm eager to learn."

At William's house, he was getting nervous that he hadn't heard from Eddie. He was sure he was going to have to spend an awkward afternoon with Jennifer. William's thoughts swirled with uncertainty, caught between the silence from Eddie and the impending social unease with Jennifer. How would they pass the time? His anxiety seemed to crescendo in perfect timing with the doorbell ringing, but things would not unfold anything like the countless scenarios he played in his head all morning. Behind the door was Danny, Leah's crush of the season, but trailing behind him was not one younger sibling but two.

"Hi, Leah," Danny began. "This is Jennifer and Matt." It wasn't much in the way of an explanation for the extra guest, but Leah didn't question it. She and Danny quickly found their way to the couch, where she had placed some blankets. She hoped they would need them. This left William with Jennifer and Matt, two people he knew from school but didn't really know at all. Worst of all, where was Eddie? If he were there, at least William would have some protection. He led his classmates - he certainly couldn't call them friends - down the hall to the lounge.

"Nice house," Jennifer said, clearly to make conversation and to be polite.

"Thanks," William said, rolling his eyes at the formalities.

"Where's Eddie?" Jennifer asked, which surprised William. "I thought you two were joined at the hip."

"We're not joined at the hip," William was trying not to be defensive with his new guests. Matt made his way into the conversation.

"Is Eddie the guy in our physics lab?" he asked his sister.

"No. He goes to Grissom," Jennifer explained.

"Oh," Matt answered, a little confused. William decided to try and change the subject.

"Who do you have for lab?" he asked, completely uninterested in the answer.

"Gershwin. You?"

"The same," the conversation was sputtering out.

"Okay," Jennifer began timidly, "I'm sure you don't, but Matt and I were wondering if you know anywhere to get some pot." It was an awkward question to ask someone you basically just met a few minutes earlier.

"We wouldn't ask," Matt added, "but our guy just moved to New York."

"Are you kidding me?" William asked with a smile. It turned out there was some common ground after all. Within fifteen minutes, the three were sitting on the backyard patio with a smoked pipe on the table.

"I can't believe you two smoke together," William said. He had come into his element and felt much more comfortable. Maybe it was because he was at home, but he rarely opened up this quickly with strangers.

"You mean because we're brother-sister?" Jennifer asked.

"Yeah. I don't smoke with my sister," he replied.

"But we're twins, so it's different," she tried to explain. Everyone laughed at this. Matt packed the pipe again, and the group chatted about nothing and laughed and lost track of time. The afternoon that William had dreaded all morning had gone by faster than he could have imagined. Before they knew it, Leah and Danny joined them on the patio.

"Alright, you two," Danny said to Jennifer and Matt. "Time to go." All three teens stood up at the patio table and started back toward the house. Jennifer paused and touched William's shoulder. He stopped and turned toward her.

"So this was fun tonight," she said with a smile.

"Yeah," William responded. Whatever confidence he found earlier had left him now that they were alone. He felt exposed and unguarded.

"Maybe we can do it again sometime. Just you and me?" she asked nervously. Was she asking him on a date? He didn't know, but he could figure that out when the time came.

"Sure," he said, still wondering what she meant by 'just you and me.'

"Okay. I'll message you online," she smiled.

"Okay. Bye," he waited on the patio until he heard the front door open and close. He snuck through the house carefully so he would not run into Leah. He didn't want to hear about her movie date with Danny. He just made it to his bedroom. However, tranquility was short-lived; downstairs, an unexpected knock echoed through the house. Had Jennifer found a reason to come back? He decided to ignore the knocking and hoped it would go away. It didn't, and a moment later, his door swung open. It wasn't Jennifer, however, it was Eddie. William was relieved.

"Where've you been all day?" He asked.

"Sorry!" Eddie apologized. "The interview went well. I got hired, and they wanted me to stay for training. I should have texted."

"Forget it," William said genuinely. "Congrats on the job. When do you start?"

"That's the thing," Eddie looked down at the floor as though he had dropped something between his shoes. "My first shift is tomorrow." William didn't mind this. "And I have to go shopping tonight for my uniform with my mom. I can only hang out a few minutes." This news struck William a little harder, but he tried not to show his disappointment.

"So when are you off tomorrow? Can we hang out at all?" William asked.

"Yes. I work ten to four, so I'll be here by four thirty," Eddie said. "By the way," he added. "I did try to call." William checked his phone and saw that he had missed several calls from Eddie.

"I'm sorry," he said. "I didn't notice. And I didn't tell you. My sister made me hang out with Jennifer Cox and her twin brother, Matt. I must have missed the calls when they were here."

"How did that happen?" Eddie asked.

"My sister is in love with their older brother, Danny, and somehow, they ended up coming over with him. We smoked weed, and I think Jennifer asked me on a date." William stopped short, and Eddie didn't react. "I don't like her," he quickly added. "Not in that way. I need to tell her in case she has the wrong idea."

"What are you going to tell her?" Eddie wanted to know.

They both thought back to the time William had told him he was gay. It was during one of their routine sleepovers in ninth grade. The room, dimly lit, held a heavy silence before William's revelation, but Eddie's acceptance and support forged an unbreakable connection, solidifying their friendship with trust and understanding. The shared vulnerability of that moment became a cornerstone in their journey, a testament to the enduring strength of their bond as they navigated the complexities of adolescence and beyond.

Eddie was staying at William's house, and William had been acting strange all night. First, he barely ate dinner, which was not like him. He was usually the type to have an extra helping, although you would never know it to look at him. Then, they were playing William's favorite racing video game after dinner, and he kept losing, which was even less like him. This was his go-to game, and he always won.

In fact, Eddie only let him pick it on rare occasions because he always lost. That night, Eddie kept winning.

Bend or Break

The last straw was when they went to sleep. As they settled into slumber, tense air lingered in the room.

Normally, they would chat about the day and talk about what they were going to do in school the following day. This was after Eddie had transferred to public school, so they each had different stories to tell and teachers to make fun of. Every day, they had so much to share with each other about how their respective days were, but on that particular night, William was silent. He kept shifting in his sheets, unable to get comfortable. Finally, Eddie had to ask.

"What's wrong tonight?" was all he could think to say. "You're acting funny. Did something happen in school?"

William sighed, and his whole body tensed. He couldn't avoid the question. In some ways, he was excited to have it over with. He wanted his best friend to know; he didn't want to keep this secret any longer, but another part of him was scared. The fear lingered like a shadow, whispering doubts about acceptance and understanding. Yet, the desire for authenticity and the hope for an unwavering friendship emboldened him to face the vulnerability of unveiling his truth. He was scared to say it out loud. No matter how close they were, he was scared it would change things between Eddie and him. He took a deep breath that trembled in his chest.

"I have to tell you something," he said in barely more than a whisper. "And I don't want you to be mad."

"You can tell me anything," Eddie encouraged. That was the cliche thing to say, but it was also true for Eddie. He couldn't think of anything his best friend could tell him that would make him mad. William took one more breath.

"I think I'm gay," a tear rolled down his pale cheek as he barely said the words out loud. He was worried Eddie hadn't heard him, and he was going to have to say it again. For a moment, Eddie didn't react. He was not expecting this news. In truth, he had always wondered if William was gay or bisexual, but he didn't give it much thought.

As the revelation settled, a mix of surprise and curiosity flickered in Eddie's eyes, quickly replaced by a reassuring warmth that spoke of unwavering support and acceptance. "But I don't like you like that." William blurted out to fill the silence and quell some of his own fears. This actually helped to diffuse the tension, but Eddie was ever the joker.

"Well, I'm a little offended," he said, but he was smiling. "I thought I was a catch." He laughed, and William shed another tear as he exhaled the biggest sigh of relief he had ever felt. His lip quivered as the breath passed. William was still too rattled to laugh, but he wasn't terrified any longer.

"Are you mad?" William asked. "Mad I didn't tell you for so long?"

"William," Eddie started with a calm that spread to his still slightly uneasy friend. "I was so scared you were going to tell me something terrible like you were moving. I don't care if you're gay. Remember what we said last year when I left Woolstead?"

"Best friends," William said with a smile, the trails of tears still on his cheeks. "No matter what."

"No matter what," Eddie confirmed. "And you better introduce me to any boyfriend of yours because if I don't approve…" he drew his finger across his neck. William smiled. In one moment, everything had changed, and nothing had changed. He and Eddie were still the same best friends they were before he had told him. Later, he would wonder why he had been nervous in the first place.

"I guess I'll tell her we should just be friends," present-day William proposed. "That's what I'm supposed to say, right?"

"Tell her whatever you want," Eddie said. "You don't owe anyone anything."

Bend or Break

Chapter Four

The next morning, William woke up to see no texts from Eddie, but he did have an alert of four new messages. They were all from Jennifer.

JenC2123 (10:56 pm): Hi William! It was so good hanging out earlier

JenC2123 (11:04 pm): We should definitely do something soon

JenC2123 (11:43 pm): Good night! Talk to you tomorrow!

JenC2123 (11:45 pm): It's supposed to be nice out. Maybe we can go to the park.

William closed his phone. He didn't want to deal with this so early in the morning. He pulled the blanket over his head and went back to sleep until he couldn't refuse the new day any longer. The cocoon of warmth offered a temporary escape, shielding him from the demands of daylight and the complexities that awaited in the waking world. The messages from Jennifer were swimming in his head. He wasn't used to anyone noticing him, so being singled out by a girl who wanted to spend time together was not in his comfort zone. Wanting to postpone responding to her, he chose to message Eddie instead, wishing him good luck on his first shift.

After pacing the house and trying to concentrate on his history assignment, he couldn't avoid the situation any longer. The weight of unresolved tension hung in the air, refusing to dissipate. Finally, he confronted the looming issue, a knot of apprehension unraveling as he faced the challenges that demanded resolution. He re-read her messages. Could he just ignore them? He didn't think so. As he was drafting his response, he received another message.

JenC2123 (11:19 am): Let me know about the park today. I think Danny and Leah are doing something so we can get a ride.

William considered his response. Eddie was working today, so he did have time, and he did enjoy spending time with Jennifer. He just needed to make sure she understood where things stood.

TheWillAndOnly (11:26 am): Jennifer, hi. The park sounds good, and I would love to go with you today, but I need to tell you something.

Bend or Break

He wished he hadn't used the word love. He saw she started typing something and stopped, deciding to wait for him to continue rather than to pry. In that moment, he grappled with the consequences of his choice of words, and she, sensing his hesitation, offered a patient space for vulnerability to unfold.

TheWillAndOnly (11:27 am): I kind of got the idea when you were over that you wanted to go on a date

Still no response from her. William was getting anxious with each message. He could feel tiny beads of sweat on his brow and the back of his neck.

TheWillAndOnly (11:29 am): Well, I'm not really looking to date anyone right now.

He pressed send and waited for what felt like an eternity. Finally, she started typing.

JenC2123 (11:34 am): That's ok

JenC2123 (11:34 am): Let's still go to the park

JenC2123 (11:34 am): Just friends

She ended her message with a smiley face. William couldn't tell if she was disappointed or not, but if she still wanted to get together, it couldn't be all that bad. He pondered the ambiguity, hoping the upcoming meeting would illuminate the true nature of her feelings. He showered and looked through his closet for something to wear to the park. What was the right outfit for going to the park with a girl who maybe likes you? Leah came into his room as he was comparing shirts.

"I heard you're going to the park with Jennifer today," she said in a sing-song voice. "Are you two dating now?"

"No way," William insisted, but Leah went on.

"Are you getting married? Do you have matching tattoos?"

"Get out!" William shouted and threw one of the shirts at her. Instead of leaving, she caught the shirt, came in, and sat on the bed.

"What?" William wondered as she stared at him awkwardly.

"You have to tell her," Leah began. "If you aren't interested, you have to tell her."

"Who says I'm not interested," William asked back. His rebellious side overtook his senses at this time. He could have said he had already told Jennifer, but he didn't want to give his sister the satisfaction. She closed her eyes calmly.

"William. I'm your sister, and I love you. I see the way you are with people, and I see the way you are with Eddie. You don't have to tell me anything you don't want to, but you owe it to Jennifer to not hurt her feelings," William's eyes welled with tears, but he held them back from cascading down his cheeks.

"I'm not in love with Eddie," he blurted out before his brain could stop his mouth. Leah didn't say anything. "We've been best friends our whole lives, is all," he insisted.

"And," Leah coaxed. Suddenly, everything William had never said came cascading from his lips.

"And if anything, we've ruined each other for dating. We have so many jokes and memories. Who else is going to be that fun to be around?" He knew he could never explain in a way she would understand.

Chapter Five

Danny drove with Leah in the front seat next to him, and Jennifer rode in the back with William. Jennifer was smiling and kept meeting William's eyes and looking away. It felt flirtatious, but it could have been nerves. As the car hummed with anticipation, William couldn't decipher whether it was the thrill of a new friendship or if there was something more behind her looks. After all, they had only been together once before and never alone.

The younger pair was dropped off at the park, which was a huge wooded area. It was much closer to a national park than a little city park where you could see the surrounding traffic lights from the center. They walked past the ranger's shack and chose a short trail to walk.

After a short distance, they came to a picnic pavilion. Really, it was just an old wooden picnic table with a cast iron grill next to it. William sat at the table, and Jennifer sat on the table with her feet on the bench. This reminded William of Eddie. He packed the pipe with marijuana and handed it to Jennifer.

Bend or Break

"Be my guest," he said as she took the pipe and lighter. Ten minutes later, the pipe lay on the table, now filled only with ash. Jennifer lay on her back on the picnic table. William was still sitting on the bench; her head was before him where his dinner plate would have been at home. He wondered how she wasn't getting splinters in her back from the old weather-worn table. Jennifer was really high on this *new stuff* that Phillip was selling. Her hair was sprawled out on the splintery table as she spoke, going on a bit of a rant. Her animated expressions painted vivid pictures, her words meandering through topics like a playful stream. William observed the kaleidoscope of emotions on her face, from euphoria to contemplation. William didn't catch every word or follow every tangent, but he did his best to keep up. Amidst the haze, William wondered if this moment would linger in the folds of their memories.

"All I'm saying is I'm not going to submit to every social rule and act a certain way simply because it's the right way to act. I mean, who makes the rules anyway?" This was a tangent William could follow, and he agreed entirely, although what adolescent does not at some point?

"I agree," he added. "I don't want to offend anyone, but every little nicety and empty 'how do you do?' just grates at my soul." She raised an eyebrow at this. Perhaps his language was a bit stronger than hers. Her ramblings continued.

"My brother doesn't get it," she didn't specify which brother, but William assumed she meant her older brother, Danny, with whom his sister was no doubt flirting at this very minute. William thought that Jennifer and Matt had a good relationship based on the single afternoon he'd spent with them. He hadn't been paying close attention, and he didn't know what Jennifer was saying that her brother didn't get. All sorts of things, he supposed, from the perspective of a teenage girl.

In the midst of her stream of consciousness, at some point, she put her hand on his, which was resting on the table. She did it casually, but William noticed she stopped talking so fast. After a moment, she turned her head, and their eyes met in an uncomfortable lock. She opened her mouth to speak, but William spoke first.

"I'm gay," he said flatly. It was just a simple fact. He might as well have said, "That's an oak tree." Surprisingly, she didn't react much at first. Surprisingly, neither did he. Her hand remained on his, their eyes still locked. Then, almost simultaneously, they sighed. His was the relief of saying something out loud. He was sure his parents knew. His sister, too, based on their conversation. He had always known, but he was going to divulge that soon enough. Her sigh, however, carried a complexity, hinting at unspoken layers beneath the surface.

"Are you sure?" she asked. They both laughed, although they didn't know why. "I'm sorry. That was a stupid question." They laughed again.

"Get them all out," he said, "It's a one-time offer." Suddenly, some barrier was lifted from between the two of them. The tension was gone, and they were both glad for it.

"Are you sure?" she asked again, and again they both laughed. This time, she was referring to the questions.

"I'm sure," he confirmed. "Ask anything you want." The first words to escape her lips were not a question, but they came out as softly as her breath, barely spoken at all.

"Matt thought so," she mused, almost unaware the words were said at all. William did not react to this. He wasn't sure he could have if he wanted to.

"Is Eddie your boyfriend?" was her first question.

"No!" he insisted. "We're best friends. Always have been. Nothing more, nothing less."

"Have you ever kissed a boy?" She was stacking questions in her head now.

"No."

"Have you ever kissed a girl?"

"No."

"Then how do you know you're gay?" he knew this question was coming. It was the question he'd asked himself years earlier. He had been through many stages of his sexual discovery, and unquestionably among those stages were the *Am I Really Gay* phase and the *Is It Okay To Be Gay* phase. He passed through these stages fairly quickly, realizing the answer to both questions was *yes*. These were facts that he had established and accepted a long time ago, but he'd never put it into words. You never took the time to think about why chocolate ice cream was your favorite flavor. When asked 'why is it your favorite?'

the answer was invariably, 'it just is.' This was how he felt about being gay. He just was.

"I just know," was the best he could do for now.

While the questions continued, they were generally easy, and William's mind wandered. He found himself thinking of the time he met Eddie. They were in second grade at recess. The class was playing dodgeball, and of course, the largest two boys were team captains. They took turns calling names until the only two boys left were William and Eddie, marking the beginning of a connection that would endure far beyond the elementary school playground.

"Okay. Those are the teams," one of the large boys announced. William and Eddie were left out. William was not athletic and knew why he wasn't chosen, but Eddie was simply new. He hadn't committed a crime and didn't deserve to be ostracized. The two boys walked the track together that surrounded the field where everyone else was playing without them. When they came to where the teacher was standing, he asked, "Why aren't you boys with the others?"

"We don't want to play with them," William said unconvincingly.

"Okay, but if you change your mind, you can go back over," the teacher's words of encouragement were interrupted by a red rubber ball connecting with William's nose. The red of the ball was met with the red of his blood. Tears came next. The teacher ran over, picked him up, and shuffled away to the nurse's office. Eddie followed and was allowed to stay with him while the nurse held cotton over his nose until the bleeding stopped.

"Do you want me to call you mother, or do you think we can stay the rest of the day?" the nurse asked.

"I'm okay," young William answered.

"Alright," she responded. "I'm going to phone your mother so she's not surprised when you get home."

"She's not home," William said meekly.

"Oh. are you," the nurse began, but Eddie spoke over her.

"He's staying with my family," he said and gave a sideways glance to William as if to say, "It'll be alright. We'll look after each other."

"Very well," she said. "You two get back to class." That night, William slept at Eddie's house for the first time, although their parents had never met. It was the first sleepover for each of them.

In the present day, William snapped back to reality and realized Jennifer was done questioning him. She had repacked the pipe with marijuana and was offering it to him.

"Can I offer this as a peace pipe?" she asked and then smacked herself in the forehead. "That was so cheesy. I mean, I want us to be friends."

A few miles from the park where William and Jennifer smoked, although it seemed like a world away, was Eddie and his cohort of taco slingers. For most shifts, there were two people working the cash registers, two people preparing the food, and one person manning the drive-through. Today, Eddie was fortunate enough to work with Ella, who was his favorite coworker so far. As it turned out, she and some of the other workers also attended Grissom High School. They were even in some of the same courses, although not the same period. Eddie was sure after the break that they would have lunch together. He was working the register today, which meant there was a decent chance he could get through his shift without being covered in salsa or queso.

Back in the woods, Jennifer and William had finished smoking and were getting along very well. The shared experience seemed to foster an easy connection, creating a moment of simple, unspoken understanding.

"Would it be okay if you introduced me to your weed guy?" Jennifer asked. "Like Matt said, our guy moved recently, and we've been out of luck."

"I'll double-check with my guy and send you his number," William said.

"Thanks. It's been such a hassle," she began but stopped mid-sentence to the sound of rustling leaves behind her. Her eyes widened as she saw the uniform of a park ranger getting closer. The vibrant hues of the forest seemed to dim in the wake of authority. A nervous energy fluttered in the air, and anticipation held its breath as the approaching figure signaled an unexpected turn in their woodland adventure. Had he seen them smoking weed? She was paranoid and worried she was going to park jail. William saw the ranger but kept his composure.

"Afternoon," the officer began like he was a sheriff walking into a saloon. "How are you two doing?"

"Fine, sir. How are you?" William responded in his most polite and respectful tone.

"Alright. How did you all get down here?" the ranger asked.

"We took the path," William said. It sounded like he was being smart when he said it, but how else could they have gotten there? At least he resisted the sarcastic response of saying they repelled from helicopters with SWAT gear. That would not have gone over well.

"That path?" the ranger asked, pointing down the way they had come.

"Yes, sir," William said. It felt like a trick question. Jennifer was nervously observing the interaction from her vantage point, sitting up on the table again, and she was keeping quiet as long as she could.

"So you walked past the large NO TRESPASSING sign," the ranger said. It wasn't quite a question or a statement, but William knew he better respond.

"I didn't see a sign," he said and looked at Jennifer. "Did you?" She shook her head, still not wanting to speak unless absolutely necessary. William looked back to the ranger. "We didn't see a sign."

"What are you doing out here?" the ranger continued his questions. Between Jennifer's and the ranger's, William had had just about enough questions for one afternoon.

"Just enjoying nature," he said, mostly honestly.

"Shouldn't you be in school?" the ranger asked.

"It's spring break, sir," William was careful to keep his respectful tone.

"Right. Do you have your IDs on you?" the ranger requested. The teens produced their learner's permits. Jennifer handed hers to William, and he handed them both to the ranger, who looked them over carefully and then handed them both back to William.

"Is your father James Blake?" he asked.

"Yes, sir," William replied. He couldn't imagine how the ranger knew his father, but it seemed to be an advantage in this instance.

"I see," he replied. "Well, you two need to head on back out of here, okay?" They followed the ranger up the path and turned left toward the entrance to the park while the ranger turned right, deeper into the woods. When he was out of range of their talking, Jennifer spoke first.

"That was amazing," she said. "He had no idea." William's heart was racing, but he pretended to play it cool for his new friend.

"Of course not," he said casually. "You just have to know how to deal with cops." She saw right through his bravado, and they both burst into laughter.

Chapter Six

William wanted Jennifer to meet Eddie, so the next day, after Eddie's shift at work was over, he arranged for them both to come over. He wondered how his newest friend would get along with his oldest friend.

The prospect of blending two separate worlds, each carrying its unique dynamics and history, intrigued and excited him. As thoughts wove between the past and present, he pondered the potential for camaraderie or collision, unsure of the harmonious or discordant notes that might emerge from this convergence of friendships.

It seemed strange to him that they hadn't met yet. He felt like he had two separate parts of his life, two secrets from each other that he was afraid to share. At the same time, he was excited to bring these two friends together. Could they, in time, form a circle of friends, as he had seen so many times in school and envied? He didn't want to get ahead of himself. Jennifer arrived first, and they went to the lounge to wait for Eddie. William kept an eye on his phone, and finally, he got the text telling him Eddie was on his way.

"What do you two like to do?" she asked.

"We mostly just hang out and do nothing," William said.

"Sounds like fun," she rolled her eyes with a smile.

"We always manage to find something fun to do. Some adventure."

"Oh, if we're going to smoke and go on an adventure, we should call my brother. Matt is so much fun," Jennifer suggested.

"Sounds good to me," William was thinking of the circle of friends they might become. Just then, Eddie came through the door. He hadn't knocked on the front door of William's house in years.

"Hey! William!" he was excited to see his friend after what felt like a long day at work. He didn't have a lot to compare it to, but it felt good to be done with his shift and able to relax. At first, he barely noticed Jennifer was there.

"How was work?" William asked. It was the first time he asked Eddie that question, and it felt funny leaving his lips. It felt like a shift somehow.

"It was great," Eddie started. "I worked with Ella again. She's really fun." Jennifer found herself wondering if Eddie had feelings for the girl he was talking about. He certainly seemed interested. She wondered why she didn't ask William if Eddie was gay the day before at the park. She supposed she had invaded his privacy enough. If they all became friends, she would find out when the time was right. Realizing she had drifted off in her thoughts, she came back to reality in time for her introduction, collecting herself with a quick, apologetic smile before engaging with the present moment.

"Anyway, this is Eddie," William was saying, "and this is Jennifer." Although they had technically met at Ron Silvan's ninth birthday party, they both said, "Nice to meet you."

"Well," Eddie said in an excited tone, "after a few days of tips, I was going to pay Phillip a visit."

"Nice!" William congratulated him. "We were just there this afternoon. I introduced Jennifer. But I can go with you if you want." Eddie felt a touch of warmth in his cheeks. Was he jealous that Jennifer was invading what felt like his and William's own little world, or was he embarrassed that William asked if he needed an escort to buy some weed around the corner? Maybe it was something else entirely. William continued, "Jennifer's brother is coming over, so we can all hang out."

"Sounds good," Eddie said and left the room to head to Phillip's house a few blocks away. It was twilight as he left William's house, and the sky was a peachy color streaked with coral. The streetlights would not come on for another ten minutes or so. Eddie hummed a tune as he went. He was musically inclined, having discovered his skills in middle school band class. None of the elective courses interested him and William, so they chose band class, which sounded easy. For Eddie, it was. He played the French horn but easily switched to the trumpet. He was not in the high school marching band, but he had picked up playing the guitar over the years, and he was pretty good. William, on the other hand, had absolutely no musical inclination. The harmonies and melodies that resonated with others seemed like an elusive language beyond the grasp of his understanding. He tried just about every instrument in middle school. Drums were the most disastrous, as his rhythm was worse than his pitch. He struggled through two years of playing the tuba, which

Eddie said was the easiest instrument. William didn't find it easy, but with Eddie's help, he managed.

Eddie walked the pathway up to Phillip's front door. There were no lights on, and the whole neighborhood was looking a bit ominous in the dusk. Shadows clung to the edges of houses, and the quiet streets whispered with the mysteries of the approaching night, adding an air of suspense to the dimly lit surroundings that heightened a sense of anticipation. He was sure the streetlights would flick on at any second. Still humming, he knocked three times on the black door. After a pause, the metal cover of the peephole was heard sliding, then the chain. The door opened a crack, and Phillip stuck his nose out, his face mostly hidden by shadows in the low light.

"Hi," Phillip said blankly. Even in the dimness, Eddie noticed him glance past as if he were looking for William to be with him. He had never come alone, so he supposed it wasn't meant to be offensive.

"Hey," Eddie said back with all the confidence he could muster. It wasn't much, but he stood tall at the open door of the house where he spent his childhood years. Here he was, like a kid on Halloween, knocking on the door like a stranger. But it wasn't trick or treat; he was a paying customer.

"Uh," Phillip looked around once more. "What's up?"

"Nothing," Eddie began and decided he better get to business. "Wondering if you had anything good."

"Come in," Phillip said. He opened the door enough for Eddie to walk through and then closed it behind him. "Come with me," he added. Eddie realized he'd never been in Phillip's room upstairs. Well, he had been in there years earlier when it was his brother's room, but not since Phillip and his family moved in. Eddie was happy that Phillip hadn't moved into his old room. It would have been too strange to see someone else's belongings in his old space. This was already strange enough. Eddie followed Phillip upstairs, past his old bedroom, and into Phillips. He stood just inside the doorway while Phillip went to his desk.

"How much?" Phillip asked.

"Um," Eddie hesitated. William always bought the weed. He was out of his element and felt like Phillip could tell, the way a dog could smell fear. "What are the prices?"

"Just tell me how much you want to spend," Phillip said impatiently. Eddie wondered what he could possibly be keeping him from and struggled not to roll his eyes.

"Twenty?" Eddie said with no confidence at all.

"Twenty?" Phillip asked back as though he were offended.

"Is that a bad amount?" Eddie asked innocently. He didn't know why Phillip was being so confrontational, but he wished he hadn't come. Or he wished William was there.

"Nope," Phillip said and shuffled in his desk drawer. He walked back to Eddie at the door and handed him a small plastic bag. He kept his hand out, waiting for Eddie to pay him, which he promptly did. Phillip opened the door and raised his eyebrows to say, "Okay. we're done here." The message was received.

Back at William's house, Eddie shared his new greenery and vented about his experience with Phillip.

"He's just a jerk," William tried to console. "You said it yourself. If he didn't sell weed, I definitely wouldn't be his friend." That word struck Eddie. Was William actually friends with Phillip? He didn't think so, but the image of them sitting together in the Woolstead cafeteria made him angry for some reason.

"That's so strange," Jennifer mused. "He was so nice to me when William introduced us." She didn't realize that her comment was basically the opposite of what William had just said, but both the boys did. William laughed, but Eddie was upset.

"He just doesn't like me," he went on. "And I don't know what I ever did to him." He didn't know why he was so worked up, but he didn't want to ruin the night. He especially didn't want to meet someone new. He decided to leave before Matt arrived.

"I think I'm going to go home," he said in barely a whisper.

"Oh, don't let him ruin your night," William said.

"No, it's not that," Eddie said, although he knew his lie wasn't convincing. "I'm working in the morning, and I'm not up for much of an adventure tonight. I'll call you after my shift tomorrow."

"Where do you work?" Jennifer asked, hoping to distract him from his misadventure and convince him to stick around.

"Taco Plaza on Warwick," he told her.

"Oh, cool. I want a job, but my mom won't let me until next summer," she added. Then, a smile grew on her face as she realized something. "Wait. Is that the place where they sing for tips?" Eddie closed his eyes and groaned.

"Yes. We sing for tips, but hey, at least I get some tips," he tried to rationalize. All three laughed. Eddie's smile faded first. "Alright. I'm going to go," he said. Jennifer's ploy had worked momentarily, but not as well as she had hoped.

"Okay. Be safe. I'll see you tomorrow," William said. He didn't want Eddie to leave. He was fantasizing about the circle of friends, the four of them. Tonight, it would only be three. He decided that was okay. The whole circle of friends couldn't always be together. He was getting ahead of himself already. The set of four would go through a lot more difficulties before they might consider themselves a crew.

"Nice to see you," Jennifer said with a smile. "Hope we can all do something soon."

"Nice to see you," Eddie mumbled and left for the night.

"You think he's okay?" Jennifer asked

"He'll be fine," William said, still thinking about the group he was certain they were going to grow into.

Twenty minutes later, Matt arrived. Rather than ringing the doorbell or knocking, he called Jennifer when he arrived.

"That's Matt," she announced when she hung up the phone. "He's here." William smiled, wondering why Matt didn't just knock. When he joined them, the mood felt really natural, not forced, the way William felt most of the time around other people. William hadn't noticed when they were all together the first time, but it struck him that although they were twins, Matt and Jennifer did not look much alike. They shared the same big hazel eyes with long eyelashes, but Matt's face was softer, more delicate. His nose was small, and his cheeks soft. Jennifer's structure was thinner and more bony. She had a pointed nose, and her cheekbones were more distinct.

Despite the familial similarities, their individual features painted a unique portrait for each. Matt's gentleness reflected in the curvature of his features, while Jennifer's angularity spoke of a different kind of grace.

As they stood side by side, the subtle contrasts in their appearances echoed the intricate symphony of genetics, weaving a visual tapestry that showcased their shared lineage and distinct individuality. William didn't think it was just her makeup. Was she even wearing any?

"Jennifer tells me you saved the day at Shoreline Park last week," Matt said. He sounded rather impressed.

"I really didn't do anything," William insisted, but Jennifer jumped in and told the story like he was George himself slaying the dragon.

"You should have seen it," she was giddy. "He's just being modest."

"I really didn't do anything," he repeated. He started to blush, but he was also grinning with delight at being the hero of the silly story.

"No way," she went on. "He dealt with the cop like it was nothing. I was so stoned, I couldn't even speak when he walked up."

"Sounds like you're good to have in a pinch," Matt said with a smile as his eyes met William's. "By the way, thanks for setting us up with Phillip. He's great." Jennifer cringed, and Matt knew he had said something he shouldn't have. "What happened?" he asked as he looked from William to Jennifer.

"He wasn't very nice to Eddie earlier," Jennifer said.

"It's fine," William interjected. "I should have gone with him. It's my fault."

"How is it your fault?" Matt wanted to know

"Well, it's not really," William conceded. "Phillip just thinks he's better than anyone who goes to public school. Like it makes any difference."

"Seriously?" Matt asked, not expecting an answer. "Why do you still associate with him then?"

"That's a good question," William said as though he had never considered it. "We should find a new dealer."

Chapter Seven

The next morning was marvelous. It was one of those *sun is shining, birds are chirping, not a care in the world*, perfect kind of days. At least, that's the way William felt. He woke up with a smile on his face. Sure, he had a best friend for years, and nothing was threatening that (as far as William could foresee), but he never had friends. He never had a group of friends, a chosen family of people to care about, and those who cared about him. He was definitely getting ahead of himself, envisaging connections that were yet to be formed and the warmth of bonds that remained unexplored.

Matt hadn't even met Eddie yet, and he was half sure Jennifer still had a crush on him. This morning, the plan was to meet Matt and Jennifer at their house, and the three would go to the lake for an adventure. William wished Eddie could go, but he was working. No matter, he would meet up with them after his shift, and William was sure the four of them would find some sort of trouble to get into.

Eddie was having the opposite morning. He woke up late and barely got to Taco Plaza before his shift started.

Bend or Break

Things went downhill from there. Someone named Lilly had called in sick, so he was the only person working the cash registers, and it was busy. They had recently started serving breakfast, and the discount breakfast burritos had become a hit with the local timber yard workers. He must not have been the only one having a bad morning. It seemed everyone was in a big rush or had an attitude.

After making change for a timber yard worker who ordered three breakfast burritos and a Mountain Dew to drink, a rather large woman stepped up as the next customer in line. Her hair was gathered in a tight, greasy ponytail, and her face was splotched with red. She looked unpleasant even before she opened her mouth. When she did, Eddie found out that sometimes you can judge a book by its cover. She spoke with a thick Massachusetts accent.

"Last time I was here, I ordered," she began, but here and ordered had no Rs to be heard. "Three number two combos," she continued almost incomprehensibly to Eddie, "and they came out all wrong."

"I'm sorry, ma'am," was all Eddie could think to say. He didn't know what she expected him to do about an order that was wrong in the past. He tried to assure her, "We'll make sure we get your order right today."

"I'm not leaving until I check," she went on. Lost in thought about William, Eddie yearned for his companionship. He thought about Jennifer and tried not to be jealous. William was allowed to have other friends, after all. Maybe he ought to have a few new friends as well. It sounded better in theory. The idea of actually spending time with anyone new sounded terrible, in fact.

Back at Jennifer and Matt's house, the twins were flanking William on the oversized couch on which they sat. They didn't live in William's neighborhood but one of similar affluence a mile north of Woolstead Academy. There were three glasses of iced tea in front of them on the glass coffee table, perched atop red cloth coasters, which all had darker red rings from the condensation. Matt's was mostly empty, as was William's, but Jennifer hardly seemed to have drunk any at all. William was almost tempted to drink some of hers, as it was so refreshing, and he found himself thirsty.

"Let's go to the river," Jennifer suggested. She raised her eyebrows and looked at the boys beside her.

"After lunch," Matt insisted, "I'm starving. Will, don't you want to have lunch before we go?"

Will? No one called him Will, and he usually hated nicknames for himself. He was never Will or Willy as a child. It was always William. He liked the sound when it came from Matt's lips. He liked the idea of being Will to him, and he took a large gulp of iced tea, hoping the cold beverage would stop him blushing. He wasn't the only one who caught the nickname. Jennifer had cocked her head and was looking at Matt, confused, her hazel eyes searching for clarity. Was her expression because he called William 'Will' or because he invited him to stay for lunch?

At the Taco Plaza, things were not improving for Eddie. As he was finishing with the unpleasant woman from Massachusetts, the previous customer came back to the counter.

"You gave me the wrong change," he charged. "I was supposed to get thirteen dollars and eighty cents, and you only have me forty cents." He held out a crumpled receipt with the change in his hand. Eddie could feel everyone in the room watching him, and he knew his coworkers in the kitchen could hear his mistake. He was embarrassed. *How simple is it to count out the correct change?* he thought to himself.

"One second, sir," he said shyly. "I'll be able to re-open the register after the next order." The man huffed with impatience. It occurred to Eddie that the man's order was not ready yet, so he really had nowhere to be. This didn't quell his embarrassment.

"Here. There's a trick," Eddie heard from over his shoulder, and a wave of relief washed over him. It was Ella. She was his savior. She touched two spots on his cash register, and the change drawer popped open with a *ching*.

"Thank you," he mouthed, then turned back to the customer to provide the correct change. "What are you doing here?" he asked Ella before greeting the next person waiting in line. Ella was tying her apron behind her back and clipping on her nametag.

"Sam called and said Lilly called out, so I'm here to save the day," she smiled and stood with her fists on her hips like a superhero. They both smiled and then got back to work.

At the dining room table across town, William found himself sitting between Matt and Danny, with Jennifer and their mother across and their father at the head. The setup felt way too formal for a quick lunch before the river, but it was harmless enough. The room bathed in sunlight, and William kept catching a glare off the family portrait above the fireplace. The golden hues danced on the glass, creating an unexpected ambiance for what started as a simple lunch.

Jennifer's mother brought in a platter of chicken salad sandwiches and a bowl of mixed fruit. She handed the platter of sandwiches to William and set the bowl of fruit on the table in front of him.

"I hope you like chicken salad, dear," she said, but what she really meant was, "We're having chicken salad." William laughed to himself but kept a straight face.

"Of course," he said. "Thank you, ma'am."

"How polite," she smiled and winked at Jennifer like they had a secret. "I'll get some more tea for everyone."

"So William," Mr. Cox said, "Jennifer tells us you plan on going off to the JSB after Woolstead."

"Yes, sir."

"Taking after your father?" Mr. Cox asked with a smile. "Another business tycoon in our midst?"

"That's still over two years away," William tried to play it down.

"You know Danny just got accepted to the School of Business at Chilton," Mr. Cox went on.

"I start this fall," Danny added with his usual brevity.

"Well, I guess we're going to be rivals," William joked.

"Looks like we're not going to become friends after all," Matt joked back. Everyone laughed at this, and the lunch continued very smoothly. What started for William as feeling like he was meeting the parents of a nonexistent significant other ended up as a pleasant afternoon. Afterward, as he analyzed the encounter, he wondered if Jennifer had intended it to be more than it was. She had exchanged that glance with her mother.

On the other side, within an hour of Ella's arrival at the Taco Plaza, the line had subsided, and the craziness of the morning rush was gone. It was really just the end of the breakfast crowd, but the timing made it seem like Ella had really saved Eddie's tail. They were working through a list of duties that needed to be performed during the slow times, but it was better than dealing with grumpy guests.

Eddie restocked the napkins and hot sauce packets while Ella swept the dining room.

"Thanks so much," Eddie said. "We'd still have a line out the door if you didn't show up."

"Don't tell anyone," Ella began and looked around as though she was going to tell a secret. "But I'm only here for the money." They both laughed. "Are you working a double today?" she asked. "If so, I'm here 'til close, too."

"Yeah, double," Eddie confirmed. The idea of spending the rest of the afternoon and evening together sounded really nice, even if it was while working.

"It's a long shift," she said.

"That's okay," Eddie replied, "bigger paycheck."

"Well, if you have any energy left, Pete's throwing a party tonight," she said. "Have you worked with Pete yet?"

"Not yet," Eddie confirmed. "I don't want to crash his party if we've never met."

"Oh, don't worry," she said. "Everyone from here's going. Besides, you'll meet eventually, and it'll be a good chance for you to see everyone outside of work."

"Sounds like fun," Eddie was actually feeling a little excited. "Do you guys party a lot?"

"Not like every night, but we hang out a lot," she said. "It's easy. You work a shift together; you hang out."

"Okay. I'll come," Eddie said. "As long as you'll be there." They both smiled.

"Here, I'll give you my number," she said. Eddie took out his phone and handed it to her so she could add her contact information. After a moment, she said, "Saved," and handed the phone back.

That evening, when Eddie's shift ended, he rode his bike home and showered right away. Even when he wasn't working in the kitchen, his uniform stank of taco meat after a long shift. He forgot entirely about his plans with Ella, and he instinctively called William. The phone rang twice, three times, and went to voicemail. It was nice to hear William's voice, but he'd prefer the real thing. He remembered Ella's invitation and decided to call her.

"Hello?" she said with a bit of an accusatory tone. Who was this unknown number calling her?

"Hey, it's Eddie," he offered quickly, cooling her attitude.

"Hey! Are you coming to Pete's?" she asked. He really wanted to meet up with William. They hadn't seen each other as much lately; it was not only due to Eddie's new job. William was changing. Was he more interested in his new friends than his best friend?

"Yeah," Eddie decided he was going to the party with Ella. "Can I meet you at your place, and we can go together?"

"Sure. I'll send you my address," Eddie hung up the phone and tossed it on his bed with a smile. He rifled through his closet and chose a green polo shirt that he thought was flattering if he did say so himself. He checked his phone and saw Ella only lived about a mile away. A quick bike ride, and he'd be there. Did he still carry the smell of tacos? He didn't think so, but he assumed everyone there had the same insecurity if they worked at the Taco Plaza.

Chapter Eight

A week later, Eddie and William were back in school, but their ritual of meeting at the park was gone. Some days, Eddie had to work; other days, they would meet with Matt and Jennifer at William's house.

The circle of friends William had desired so dearly was starting to form, but it was delicate. Like fragile threads weaving together, there was a tentative promise waiting to evolve. The unspoken bonds lingered in the air, a budding connection that carried the weight of potential and the uncertainty of what lay ahead.

Things were changing. Their world was expanding, and he hoped they could keep up with the changes. They seemed mostly good so far. Each shift and transformation in their dynamics held the promise of growth, and he cherished the optimism that permeated the air as they navigated the uncharted territories of evolving friendships.

At Woolstead Academy, Matt, Jennifer, and William would meet before class to regroup for the day. On this particular day, William was half asleep as Matt had kept them up most of the night with a Stanley Kubrick film marathon. Jennifer made it through The Shining before she fell asleep during the opening credits of 2001 A Space Odyssey. Matt and William both lasted a while longer, but by three in the morning, they were all asleep. Jennifer was on Matt's bed. William was heaped in a bean bag chair, and Matt was on the floor beside him with his head slumped over. The shared fatigue spoke of a day well-lived, etching memories in the fabric of their growing bond.

"I have an English test this morning," William moaned. "Why did you keep me up all night watching 'Barry Lyndon,' the most boring movie ever made?"

"It won four Oscars!" Matt pretended to be offended by William's comments. "It's a roller coaster of emotions."

"Did it win for the longest film?" William joked

"I was asleep way before you even got to that one," Jennifer chimed in. "But I've been the victim of his movie choices my whole life."

"And next time, I get the bed," William added. "I could barely move my neck this morning."

"Oh no!" Matt threw his arms out in a dramatic gesture. "He hates the movies; the seats are uncomfortable. I bet he hated the snacks, too."

"No," William laughed. "The snacks were okay." The bell rang, indicating the beginning of first period, and the three students went in separate directions to learn various lessons for the day.

A few miles away, Eddie was meeting with his before-school posse, which consisted of Ella and Pete, who both worked at the Taco Plaza, and Brian, who had been friends with them for several years. Brian was two grades older than the rest of the group, and it showed.

Pete and Eddie were pretty scrawny, and you were lucky if you could count five peach hairs between the two of their chins, but Brian was tall, even for his age, and had broad shoulders.

By last period, his face was darkened with stubble, and a small tuft of hair could sometimes be seen between his collar bones. The subtle details painted a portrait of untamed masculinity, a rugged physique that complemented his gentle demeanor, adding a layer of intrigue to the persona he wore with an effortless grace.

Bend or Break

Ella teasingly called him the Neanderthal, but he was kind and shy despite his towering stature, and he was more interested in books than using his muscles. Eddie found himself in his usual unprepared state, just remembering he had a test the next period. "Have you guys taken the bio test yet?" he asked Ella and Pete. Although neither of them was particularly studious, they had gotten into the habit of studying together and sharing homework.

"I take it this afternoon," Pete said and put up both of his hands with fingers crossed.

"I took it yesterday," Ella said. "Make sure you know the different theories of evolution from that handout." Eddie flipped through his binder, looking for the handout, but he knew it was futile to try and cram this close to the test. He would take his chances.

"Are you guys working today?" Brian asked in his deep voice. All three confirmed they were off that afternoon, which was rare. "Want to come over to my place?" Brian continued.

"Let's do it," Eddie said. He thought about William and his new friends. He tried to imagine them as one big group, but his mind kept them separated. He didn't want to drift apart from his best friend, but he was spending so much time with Ella and Pete at work and school that they were all growing closer. He felt pulled in two directions, not wanting to disappoint or neglect anyone.

The next evening, Matt and William were found in William's lounge with the pool table. Matt was mindlessly knocking the balls with a pool cue. He wasn't very good, but he was enjoying himself. It was as if he was in his own bubble and didn't pay much heed to what was happening around him. William checked his phone and put it back in his pocket.

"Where's Jennifer?" William asked. Sometimes, she would come around without Matt, but he and William rarely got one-on-one time.

"She needed to go to the library, but she'll be by soon. Did you get that English paper back yet?" Matt asked. English was his favorite subject and the only one that came naturally. He wondered how anyone could struggle in a course on a language they'd been speaking their whole life. He wasn't an ace in his French class, but he'd only been working on that language for two years.

"Not yet," William told him. "I'm sure I did fine. Thanks for your notes."

Matt smiled. He liked being helpful to his friends when we could. Who didn't? With a smile of his own, William crossed the room to the pool table and took the cue from Matt. Matt looked confused for a moment, but he saw William smiling.

"While you might be a genius at English," William started. "You're just terrible at shooting pool." He laughed, and Matt smiled. William took a quick survey of the felt and chose a vantage point from which to take his shot. He lined up the cue and gently knocked the red-striped eleven ball into the side pocket across from where he stood.

"See? It's a piece of cake," he joked, but when he handed the pool cue back to Matt, his smile faded, and time stopped. Instead of taking grip of the cue a few inches below where William held it, he accidentally put his hand directly over William's. It was an honest mistake of misjudged distance or poor coordination, but the result was explosive. The unexpected consequence reverberated through the air.

Each boy felt a heaviness in his chest and a lightness in his head. They both felt a spark where they touched, and their hearts began to pound. The floor rumbled and then disappeared beneath them as that top-of-the-roller-coaster feeling sank into their stomachs. Their eyes locked, and Matt thought he could see the depths of the universe in William's. Neither of them had felt anything like this in their lives, and William began to feel even more lightheaded.

"Will," he heard Matt say in barely more than a whisper, and he wondered. He wondered if Matt was feeling what he was feeling. He wondered if Matt was even gay. He wondered if they were about to kiss. But while he wondered, he also knew. He knew that touching Matt's hand made it feel like nothing else in the world mattered. He knew that gazing into his eyes made everything else disappear. He knew that hearing his own name on Matt's lips was the best sound he would ever hear. He wanted to lean in for a kiss, but he was frozen in place, hand on hand, eyes unable to look away.

Suddenly, the moment ended with a tiny buzz in his pocket. All at once, the roller coaster came crashing down.

The floor was once again beneath their feet. Breath once again filled their lungs. They blinked their eyes, and the world came back into focus, the disorienting moment of suspension now a memory replaced by the reassuring stability of solid ground. The tunnel vision was clearing. They both released their grip on the pool cue, and the reverberating clank when it hit the felt snapped the boys back to reality. Surprisingly, it was not the sound of the pool cue crashing down but the separation of their hands that broke the circuit and stopped the electricity from flowing between them. Matt cleared his throat and looked around the room while William retrieved his phone from his pocket.

"Is it Jennifer?" Matt asked. He had placed his right hand on the rim of the pool table to keep his balance. His head was still spinning from the brief contact.

"No, it's Phil," William said. "Let me see what he wants." This time, it was Matt who could only hear one side of the conversation.

"Hello?" William answered the call. "Hey, what's up?" The usual teenage formalities. Then, a pause. "Oh, no. Not for me, but I appreciate it. Yeah, I'll probably be by later tonight, though, for the usual. Is that okay? Perfect. See you later." He hung up the phone and set it on the table. He was still in a daze.

"What was all that about?" Matt asked.

"Phillip has some pills he's trying to get rid of," William explained. "Some X."

"Sounds sketchy," Matt said.

"Yeah. I don't do that kind of stuff anyway," William felt he needed to say.

"Me neither!" Matt agreed eagerly. "Just a little weed." Both boys smiled and said at the same time, "Well, maybe a lot of weed." and they laughed. Their quick moment, still fresh and defined, had not changed their youthful banter. As their laughter reached its peak, Jennifer entered the room looking exasperated.

"What's the matter with you?" William inquired, eyebrows raised. She marched over to the couch, unloaded her hefty backpack, and from it retrieved what must have been a six-hundred-page novel.

"This is the matter with me," she blurted out. "Mr. Kwon is offering me extra credit, which I desperately need, but he wants me to write a report on this book before the end of the semester. William couldn't read the title from across the room, but he knew Mr. Kwon had a reputation for assigning difficult books.

"I guess we know what you'll be doing this weekend," Matt joked.

"No chance," Jennifer snapped back with a look that suggested Matt had lost his mind. "I'll get the notes online and pull something together."

"Isn't that what got you into the situation where you need extra credit in the first place?" William asked, and they all laughed.

"Shut up!" she said playfully. "Oh, and before I forget, I ran into Jacob outside the library. He's having a mid-term party this weekend. We should totally go."

"A party?" William asked shyly. He didn't like crowds, and he didn't have many friends. He would prefer a night with Eddie. A night with Matt would be okay, too. Maybe they would hold hands again. Maybe they would kiss.

"C'mon," Matt coaxed. "You have to be social sometimes."

"Do I, though?" William joked. "It's worked out fine for me for fifteen years so far."

"It's decided then?" Jennifer asked. "We're all going?" She didn't wait for a response. "Good. I'll text Jacob."

At the same time Jennifer was finding her phone in her back to text Jacob, around the corner, Eddie was with his new friends. Brian was behind the wheel of an older white car with a sun-bleached hood. Eddie rode up front while Ella and Pete sat in the back. Playing through the speakers was a song that sounded sort of Rastafarian, but Eddie got the idea the band was probably from California and had never been anywhere close to Jamaica. All the windows were rolled down, and the spring air flowed in and out.

"That's his house there on the left," Eddie said, pointing to Phillip's house. He nearly said, "That's *my* house," even though it had been almost three years since he lived there. He was momentarily pulled into his own memory and vanished for the five seconds it took Brian to turn the car into the driveway.

Bend or Break

He was twelve years old, about to finish seventh grade, and everything was perfect. His life actually hadn't changed much in the years since, besides the move. Back then, he went to school and spent time with William, and that was about it. He didn't need anything more. The company of William was enough for him.

One night, he was, of course, having a sleepover with William when the two boys plotted to sneak downstairs for a midnight snack. Eddie's favorite was Nutty Buddies, while William favored a fistful of gummy bears. Eddie thought they were like little rubber bullets; he never understood how William could stomach them. Naive as they were, they forgot that adults often do not go to sleep until well after midnight. That was the case on this night, and as they strode the stairs, they overheard Eddie's parents talking downstairs. They never fought, and he wouldn't call this a fight, but their voices were distressed if not raised. The boys stopped on the stairs to listen.

"Are you even listening to me?" his dad was asking. He didn't sound angry. There was something else in his voice. Sadness. Sadness and desperation. Eddie hadn't heard his father speak like that before.

"I'm listening," his mom confirmed. "It's only one deal. How could it go so wrong? Aren't there other deals, Daniel?"

"This was *the* deal," he emphasized. "We've been working on it for almost a year."

"And what about everyone else?" she demanded to know. "They can't fire the whole department over one deal gone bad."

"It was my deal," he explained. "I brought it to them. I engineered it. We were that close." Eddie could imagine his father holding his thumb and pointer a millimeter apart.

"Look," his mother sounded more stern. "We can move across town. We can sell the cars. We can even pawn my jewelry, but we're not taking him out of Woolstead.

"I know you think he's getting a better education, but public school," he started to argue back.

"You think it's about his education? I'm talking about William," she said. "I'm talking about the only friend Eddie's ever had. Do you know what it's going to do to him?"

"I'll know more by the end of the week, and no matter what, he'll be able to finish the year," he said, but it wasn't much of a consolation. It was already March, and by September, Eddie and William would be neither neighbors nor classmates.

Eddie's parents put off telling him until almost June. In the meantime, he held some hope that the all-important deal had worked out or some other miracle would allow things to stay the way they were. When he heard the news, it wasn't a shock because it had already had time to settle. For all his wishing, Eddie knew he'd seen his last days at Woolstead. He wanted to yell at his father, to call him names and tell him it was all his fault, but he remembered the tone in his voice and knew there was nothing he could say that would make him feel any worse than he already did. Besides, he didn't really feel any of the hurtful things he thought to say; all he felt was numb. He didn't remember the walk to William's house.

The next memory he had after sitting at the table and hearing the news that his whole life was changing was in William's bedroom, in his arms. He was crying. Both boys were. Eddie did not have to tell William what had happened. They both remembered what they had overheard on the stairs.

"The deal?" William asked through his tears. Eddie just nodded.

"Can we promise right now," Eddie started, "that no matter what school, no matter what happens, we're always going to be best friends."

"Promise," William said.

"Promise," Eddie said out loud, but he was older now and sitting in the front seat of Brian's car. A squeal came from the engine as a belt slipped when he turned the key to the off position.

"What?" Brian asked.

"Nothing," Eddie said, realizing where they were. "Wait here. I'll be right back." He walked up to the door, but this time, there was no knock. There was no sliding of the metal peephole cover, and there was no creak of the chain. As Eddie took the first step up the stairs to the stoop, the door swung open. Phillip came out wearing baggy jeans and a black tank top undershirt. He looked mad.

"What the hell are you thinking?" he asked in a way that was both discreet enough for the front yard in the afternoon and intimidating enough to make Eddie stop where he stood, mid-stair.

"What do you mean?" Eddie was confused. He'd been before, and while Phillip never treated him like a best friend, he had been open to conducting business civilly.

"What do you mean?" Phillip mocked in a high-pitched taunt. "Can you see that car? Can you hear the thing, for Christ's sake? Those people don't blend in in this neighborhood, and neither do you. Now get the fuck out of here." Eddie was more than angry. He was being shooed away from his own old house because he wasn't good enough for a drug dealer. His anger quickly morphed into embarrassment when he turned, red-cheeked, back to his friends waiting in Brian's car.

"What happened?" Pete asked. Obviously, he had returned without transacting any business.

"Nothing," Eddie made up. "He's just not good right now." He looked down toward his lap. "Let's get out of here." As they pulled out and drove off, Ella could tell there was something more.

"You seem upset," she said. "Did something happen?"

"No, it's fine," Eddie said, but he knew this wasn't going to be a satisfactory response. "Just embarrassed I brought you out here for nothing."

"Don't worry about it," Pete jumped in. "My guy just texted me. We can swing by there." Eddie was still looking down and hoping that no one noticed he was blushing still. He looked up just in time to notice they passed by William, Matt, and Jennifer as they were leaving the neighborhood. As they passed by, William and Eddie's eyes locked. They both felt a flood of emotions. The two boys maintained eye contact until the car had passed, but in that moment when the car was closest, when William and Eddie were less than ten feet apart, a flare of passion was ignited within each of them. For William, the flare screamed, "I miss you," and the expression on his face matched. Sadness and longing wrinkled his brow. For Eddie, the flare within him declared, "I never needed you," something that would have hurt William more than he could have known. He would regret even thinking this later, but for now, he was lumping in William with Phillip as one of *them*.

William and the twins were on their way to see Phillip, and he was expecting their call. He was sitting on the front steps, the same step where Eddie had stood moments earlier and been told to leave. Phillip sat there with rolling papers in one hand and was crumbling marijuana with the other hand. As Matt, William, and Jennifer walked up, he rolled the paper around the marijuana and licked the adhesive strip.

"Hey, Phillip," William said. He had no idea of the scene that had just unfolded.

"Hey," Phillip said back. "Let's go in." He put the joint behind his ear like a pencil and led the way inside his house. Once in his bedroom, he headed for the desk while the trio waited by the door.

"Your boy Eddie is trying to get me caught," Phillip said as he sat at the desk and put his feet up.

"What do you mean?" William glanced quickly at Matt at the mention of *his boy*. What did Phillip mean by that, and how would Matt take it? Luckily, Matt didn't seem to notice. He was looking straight ahead and didn't meet William's glance.

"He rolled up in some ragged old car with a bunch of guys from Grissom that stand out around here even more than he does," Phillip explained. He wasn't exactly blaming William.

"I'll talk to him next time I see him," William said. "Although it's been a few days."

"I think he got the message," Phillip said with a smile. William wondered what he meant by that.

"Don't be mad at me," William said, far from pleading.

"No," Phillip said with a drawn-out O. "You're cool. And our mutual new friends." He added that last part with a smile and gestured to Matt and Jennifer. "How much do you want today?" Down to business.

Chapter Nine

That Wednesday, Eddie had the day off from work and no homework. He wasn't even slacking off in this instance. He genuinely had no assignments to work on. His mind was wandering off to several things at the same time. Despite the new routine he was falling into with work and seeing his new friends both at school and outside school, he missed his friend. Was he starting to think of William as his old friend? The thought scared Eddie, and he shook it from his mind. He reminded himself they were best friends. Nothing would change that. In the midst of apprehension, Eddie anchored himself in the assurance that they were even more than best friends, like brothers, and shared a bond unyielding to the uncertainties ahead. Clinging to the steadfast belief that nothing would alter their profound connection, he drew strength from the enduring foundation of their friendship, a beacon in the unknown. Despite everything, he still felt confident.

Before school, he texted William that he wanted to meet up after school. "The usual spot later?" he asked. Even though it hadn't been their usual spot lately, calling it the old spot felt as awkward as calling William his old friend.

William woke up that morning feeling refreshed, the restorative embrace of a good night's sleep lingering. Empowered by the dawn's freshness, he approached the day with enthusiasm, ready to embrace challenges and savor the possibilities that unfolded with each moment in the wake of a revitalizing sleep. He rolled over in his sheets - he had a way of sleeping without disturbing them in the slightest - and turned off his alarm. He got out of bed, tucked in his seemingly unslept-in blanket, and noticed the alert on his phone. His first thought was that it might be a message from Matt. Intrigued, he reached for his phone, the anticipation of connection fueling his morning. Curiosity danced in his thoughts as he eagerly explored the potential communication that awaited him from his friend. Was he messaging William to say he felt the same fireworks when they touched, or had he messaged something else entirely? Would he blame the whole thing on William and spread a rumor around school that the homo tried to hold his hand? None of this mattered because the message was from Eddie. He wanted to meet at their spot after school. William considered for a moment, then laughed to himself. A few weeks earlier, they wouldn't have even messaged to coordinate a meeting after school. They would have done it without thinking. Reflecting on the unspoken understanding they shared once, William realized that true friends didn't need messages to coordinate meetings after school. Their connection transcended the need for explicit communication; it was an instinctive bond where actions seamlessly aligned, a testament to the depth of their friendship that went beyond mere coordination or planning. He messaged back that, of course, he would be there.

At school, Eddie met up with Pete and Ella before class. They were in the library sitting at a table while Brian was off somewhere looking for a new book to read.

"What are we doing later, gents?" Ella asked. "Want to come over to my place?"

"Yeah, sure," Pete said, and he and Ella looked at Eddie for confirmation.

"Actually, I'm going to hang out with William today," he said, unsure how his friends would react.

"Ok," Ella said. It wasn't a big deal. "He can come, too." Pete seized the opportunity to give Ella a hard time.

"Do you have a crush on the rich boy?" he teased. If they only knew, Eddie thought. He thought back to the time William cried while telling Eddie he was gay. Eddie's mind retraced the raw honesty that accompanied those tears. The memory etched a profound understanding between them, proof of their enduring friendship, built on acceptance, support, and the shared vulnerability that strengthened their bond. He thought of the time he cried while telling William he was changing schools.

"Shut up!" Ella shouted and smacked Pete in the arm with her spiral notebook. A librarian's shhh was heard from off in the distance, and all three students flinched. "I do not!" she continued in a quieter but equally insistent tone. Brian rejoined them with two new books freshly checked out.

"Are you three causing trouble?" he accused jokingly. Just then, the bell rang, and everyone stood to exit the library.

"Hang on a minute," Eddie told Ella as he touched her arm. Pete and Brian shrugged at each other and left to go to class.

"What's up?" Ella asked.

"Is it true what Pete said?" he asked, finding it difficult to look her in the eye. "Do you have a crush on William?"

"No!" she said, as exacerbated as when Pete had suggested it. "We've only met once, and besides, rumor has it you two are an item." This didn't bother Eddie in the slightest.

"We're definitely not an item," Eddie confirmed, "and I'm kind of glad to hear you don't have a crush on him." Eddie yearned for a telepathic connection with her, a silent understanding that would spare him from completing the sentence. Regrettably, such a connection eluded them, and he braced himself to articulate the unspoken, navigating the challenge of expressing thoughts that lingered in the uncharted recesses of his mind. "Because," he was now speaking one word at a time, deciding after each one if he dared continue. "I kind of," he looked at her intensely, once again hoping she would intuit the rest. "Have a crush on you?" As Eddie began speaking, he realized the unintended inflection, the statement inadvertently morphing into a question. The nuance escaped him, a subtle twist that underscored the complexity of the emotions he grappled with. The bell rang again, which meant they were now late for class.

"I do have feelings for you, Eddie," she began, and then she lowered her eyes. He was sure he was about to be rejected by the first girl he ever admitted he had feelings for. "But I'm not sure I'm ready for a boyfriend." This wasn't the bad news Eddie foresaw. "Can we take things slowly and not make a big deal?"

"We can definitely do that," Eddie said with a smile he would have been embarrassed to see on his own face. "Can Brian's party be a secret date this Friday?"

"Ok," she said and gave Eddie's hand a squeeze. "Let's go. We're going to be in trouble." The rest of the day was a blur to Eddie. His head was in the clouds.

At lunchtime, William joined Jennifer for their meal while Matt spent the time working with his science fair partner. Confronting a stark realization, he acknowledged his shortfall in the collective effort. Determined to rectify the imbalance, he recognized the imperative to invest more of himself, committing to contribute his fair share and aligning his actions with the shared responsibilities at hand. Jennifer and William ate lunch outside because the weather was so nice. They sat on the corner of a brick planter with a young but hearty birch tree.

"Are you sure you want to go to Jacob's party this Friday?" Jennifer asked.

"I'm sure it will be fine," William said. He wished Matt had bailed on his science fair partner.

"I think it's going to be pretty crowded," she went on.

"I know. I'll be ok," he said

"Because I know you don't like being around a lot of people. Don't feel like you have to go," she said. "We can do something else, you know."

"We can go," he said, "and if I decide it's too much, we can get out of there."

"Ok," she said, but she had triggered a rant.

"I just don't get why you would need more than two or three people in one place," William began. "There is no way you can talk to everyone, and it gets so loud. All I hear is chewing and laughing amplified to a deafening volume."

"I know," she said. She wanted to add, "That's why I asked!" but she didn't have the chance.

"And all the 'how's it going?' and 'how's life?' and 'how's school?'" his rant continued. "I don't care, and I know whoever is asking me doesn't care."

"I know," Jennifer offered again.

"I think I'm going to go crazy eventually," he declared to end his tirade.

"What does crazy even mean?" she asked.

"I think I'm going to be a recluse. They'll find me one day organizing piles of phone books and highlighting dictionaries."

"Don't worry," she smiled. "I'll keep you away from the phone books." William smiled back.

"You know what I mean," he said. "Do you ever feel like you're the only one who thinks the way you do?"

"No," she said flatly. "But I know if you don't want to go to the party, it's okay."

"Let's do it."

That afternoon was just like old times. William and Eddie met at their bench in the mostly empty park, enveloped by the familiar tranquility. The resonance of shared history permeated the air, and a comforting sense of continuity prevailed as they embarked on another timeless rendezvous. They smoked their weed and told each other about their days. The time that had passed did not create distance between these two. When they had smoked a second pipe, Eddie picked up on the same vibes he remembered from a year earlier when William had been tossing in his bed with a secret to tell.

"Is it good news or bad news?" Eddie asked directly. Anything big enough to keep as a secret had to be either good or bad news.

"What makes you think I have news?" William asked back.

"I've known you forever," Eddie provided as an explanation. "Now spill the beans."

"Well," William began, but Eddie did not have the patience to wait for him to find his words.

"Get to it," Eddie coaxed half-jokingly. "I have my own news to share."

"You can go first," William said. He still wasn't sure how Eddie was going to take the news that he had feelings for Matt. The unspoken tension hung between them, awaiting resolution as William braced himself for a conversation that held the potential to reshape the contours of their friendship. Did it even count as news to share until he and Matt had a chance to speak?

"Not a chance," Eddie smiled, "Now tell me so you can stop squirming like you have to pee." William reminded himself that they were best friends, but he was still worried. Was he worried that Eddie would judge him or worried that Eddie would be jealous of a shift in the allocation of his time and attention? In the end, he was worried for no reason.

"I think I like someone," he said quietly. "I think I have a crush on Matt."

"Well, duh," Eddie smiled. "You only ever talk about him, and I know you basically only put up with Jennifer to hang out with him." Then came the unavoidable question. "Is he gay?"

"I don't know," William answered honestly. "He touched my hand, I think by accident, but he also gave me a look. I don't know."

"This is great!" Eddie announced. "I'm so happy for you." Then his tone turned more serious. "What are his intentions?" They both laughed, and William was relieved to have someone to talk to about all this with. "Are you boyfriend and boyfriend?" Eddie asked.

"No. We haven't even talked about it," William said. "Really. There's nothing to tell."

"Ok. Ok. But you do have a crush?" William did not answer his questions directly. He Might not have even heard it.

"He called me 'Will,'" was all he provided for an explanation.

"No one calls you that," Eddie said with visible shock, and truly, in all the years he'd known William, he had never heard anyone refer to him any way other than his full first name.

"He does," William said with a big stupid grin on his face. His gaze was a thousand miles away. He was momentarily back in the lounge with Matt's hand clenched over his own.

"Well, that is great," Eddie went on. "I want to hear every detail." William came back to the present and gave him a sideways, confused glance. "I mean, not every detail." Then, wanting to change the subject, he turned to his own news. "Ok. I don't want to steal your thunder."

"You can borrow it," William slipped in as Eddie paused. They both laughed.

"I think I have a date on Friday," he continued, then paused for the news to sink in. He hoped William would be as happy about his announcement as he was about Will's crush on Matt, fostering an atmosphere of mutual support and celebration within their friendship.

"Do you think you have a date, or do you have a date?" William asked, making a bit of a joke, but Eddie was glad to see he was smiling.

"I have a date," he confirmed. "With Ella. We work together, and she goes to Grissom. We've been spending a lot of time together." He looked down for a moment, embarrassed to be explaining why he hadn't been with William lately. But here they were together again. It seemed the past few weeks hadn't changed anything besides their romantic situations. The core of their friendship remained steadfast, resilient to the shifts in their individual romantic landscapes.

"Congrats, Eddie," William sounded genuinely happy for his friend. "What are you doing for your date?"

"We already had plans to go to this guy's party," Eddie explained. "So we just decided to make it a date, but she doesn't want to make it a big deal, so it's kind of on the down low."

"A secret party date," William found a term for the situation Eddie was describing.

"A secret party date," Eddie repeated. Both boys were grinning. "You have a crush on a guy you're not sure is gay, and I have a secret party date." They were laughing again now.

"We're basically hopeless," William concluded.

"Hopeless," Eddie repeated.

"I might actually be going to a party on Friday, too," William said with the slightest cringe.

"I'm sorry," Eddie began. "I must have misheard you. I thought you said you were going to a party on Friday."

"I am!"

"Are you just going because Matt's going to be there?" Eddie wanted to know.

"Not just for that reason, but I was hoping we'd have time to talk about what happened," William explained.

"A crowded party full of drunk classmates might not be the best place," Eddie cautioned.

"We'll find somewhere. I don't know," William paused, overwhelmed with thoughts and emotions. "I need to know how he feels. I need to know if we're going to hold hands again, hold hands for real." Eddie could relate to the longing for William's truth. It wasn't quite desperation. He had felt a similar anxiousness before telling Ella he had feelings for her.

"I guess I better head home," William said.

"I'll walk with you. I'm headed to Phillip's," Eddie replied.

"Are you sure that's a good idea?" William asked, thinking about what Phillip had said.

"Yeah. We're cool," Eddie explained. "I shouldn't have brought those other guys with me the other day. I texted Phillip. He knows I'm coming by."

"Do you want me to go with you," William offered.

"Thanks. I'll be fine." Eddie didn't sound very confident.

"On our way," William said with a growing smile. "Let's stop for an energy drink."

When the boys entered the store, William in his Woolstead uniform and Eddie in jeans and a T-shirt, the first detail they observed was the clerk. It was a scrawny man in his early twenties with greasy hair and a dumb look on his face. His presence was accompanied by a somewhat unintelligent visage that seemed to linger persistently. As usual, Eddie took the lead. He seemed panicked.

"We need to get rid of it," he said to William frantically. "After this, we need to go to the hardware store." He looked over each shoulder like he was about to tell a secret, but really, he was making sure the clerk was paying attention. "We need trash bags, um, bleach." William got the idea of where he was going with this and dove into the ruse.

"At least a few gallons of bleach, rubber gloves, and rags," he said. This nearly made Eddie burst out laughing.

"Lots of rags," Eddie agreed as they each selected an energy drink from the refrigerator. "And some kind of saw. Is a hack saw strong enough?" They had made their way up to the counter, and the clerk scanned the drinks.

As William paid, he looked right into the clerk's eyes and asked, "Do you know the best saw for cutting through bone?" The clerk looked mortified and simply shook his head as the boys took their energy drinks and left the store. They immediately started laughing, and the walk back to William's neighborhood was as fun as any time they could remember together. The shared laughter echoed through the streets, rekindling the warmth of their enduring friendship.

Chapter Ten

Thursday passed in a blur, and before they knew it, it was the day of the parties. William woke up to find one new message on his phone. He hoped it was from Matt, but it was from Jennifer, telling him it wasn't too late to skip the party if he changed his mind. He rolled his eyes and flopped out of bed to start his day. Matt had definitely been avoiding him since the incident, as William had begun referring to it. The unspoken tension hung thick between them, casting a shadow on their interactions, leaving William yearning for resolution and a return to their former camaraderie. At lunch, Matt was either in the library or the computer lab. Although Jennifer didn't seem to notice his absence, William did.

"Are you ready for tonight?" she asked.

"I guess," he said mindlessly. "Do I need to bring beer or anything?"

"It's BYOB, so I'll get Danny to get us something," she said, then added, "wear something casual. Try to have fun."

"I'll try," William said, but he had no idea how someone tried to have fun. Either you were having fun or not, right? He didn't care if the party was fun or not as long as he got the opportunity to talk to Matt about the incident. The prospect of resolution and understanding took precedence over any potential enjoyment at the gathering.

Eddie found himself distracted during the school day as well but for different reasons. Before classes, Ella seemed different, more reserved. While he and Pete were complaining about homework and their shifts for the upcoming weekend at the Taco Plaza, Ella was quiet. Her subdued presence added a contrasting note to the lively atmosphere. She shifted her weight from foot to foot and didn't seem to make any eye contact. At lunch, she was the same. Eddie cracked a joke, and Ella looked up and laughed, but when her eyes met his, her smile faded, and she looked down at her half-eaten sandwich. Pete must have sensed the tension. He looked from Eddie to Ella, trying to break the silence.

"Are we all set for tonight?" he asked.

"Yeah," Eddie said. "I picked up some green last night."

Bend or Break

"And Brian has beer covered," Pete said. "I don't think he even gets carded anymore." This provoked a brief smile on Ella's face before whatever was troubling her returned. The fleeting moment of brightness hinted at a deeper struggle, leaving an indelible impression on those who observed the transient shift in her demeanor.

After school that afternoon, William was trying to decide what to wear. "Wear something casual," Jennifer had suggested. He chose a blue striped polo shirt and chino pants. He imagined Matt doing the same thing in preparation for the evening, then decided it was a silly thought.

Matt was not the sort of guy to spend an hour choosing an outfit. He would throw on something quickly and still look amazing. William marveled at Matt's innate ability to exude charm effortlessly, an aspect of his friend's personality that never failed to captivate those around him. William was lost in his thoughts when he got a text from Jennifer. She was asking if he wanted to come by her house before the party, and they could all go together. He responded that he did. This was the perfect opportunity to talk to Matt. If it went well, they would have fun at the party together. If it didn't go well, he could come home and wallow. He checked the clock. Two hours until he needed to leave.

Meanwhile, Eddie had been texting Ella all afternoon. He was asking what was wrong and offering to talk if she wanted to. Eventually, she responded, telling him that they would talk at Brian's party later. That felt ominous, but at least she said something. At least she had acknowledged the impending conversation, dispelling the silence that had lingered between them.

When William arrived at Jennifer and Matt's house, he felt cheated. Matt wasn't even there. "He said he'd meet us at Jacob's," Jennifer explained casually. "It's just us for now." She smiled, and William thought he saw her wink when she said it. He must have imagined the wink. "You carry the beer," she added with a smile and handed William a backpack. He guessed it was one of Danny's that he didn't use anymore. It was heavy with the weight of twelve cans. While William and Jennifer prepared to leave her house and walk to Jacob's across town, Eddie was walking with Pete and Ella to Brian's. Ella was still quiet and acting somewhat uncomfortable around him.

The palpable unease cast a noticeable shadow over their interactions. Eddie thought he knew why, and he got the chance to ask when Pete's phone rang.

"It's my dad," he said and answered the call.

"Hey," Eddie said to Ella when he knew Pete wouldn't hear. "You've been acting strange since the library the other day. It's ok if you don't like me back. I just wanted you to know how I felt." She looked to Pete to make sure he couldn't overhear.

"I like you a lot, Eddie," she started hesitantly. "I'm just not sure I'm ready for a boyfriend."

"I completely understand," he said, and she sighed with relief. "Now, can you please relax so we can go enjoy this party as friends?" She smiled as Pete rejoined them, and they continued their way to Brian's house.

So far, neither Eddie nor William was having the night they expected. Eddie wanted this to be a date or even a secret party date. He tried to mask that he was feeling slightly rejected, but Ella had become a good friend. He was still eager to spend time with her, even if it wasn't in a romantic way. Despite the discomfort, Eddie remained eager to spend time with Ella, recognizing the value of their connection beyond romantic implications. His genuine desire for companionship overshadowed the strained atmosphere, fostering hope for a renewed rapport.

William was trying to hide that he was simultaneously disappointed that he hadn't had the opportunity to speak with Matt at his house before the party and anxious about the party itself, and still, a small part of him couldn't stop thinking about what-ifs. What if Matt felt the same thing he had in the lounge a few days earlier? What if they were going to fall in love and be boyfriends and go on romantic dates? By the time he had run through all these thoughts a few dozen times, he and Jennifer had made it to Jacob's house. They could hear music from inside, and Jennifer was holding his hand, trying to pull him along. The rhythmic beats served as a backdrop to the tension. Amidst the turmoil, he maintained a facade of composure.

"C'mon," she said with a smile. "Give it a try. Like you said, we can always leave if you don't have fun." William wasn't hesitating for the reasons Jennifer thought.

"Is Matt here yet?" It wasn't exactly what he had meant to say, but those were the words that came out.

"I'm going in," Jennifer said, seeming frustrated. "If you want to wait out here for Matt, be my guest." She dropped his hand and marched to the front door of the large house.

In the three seconds during which she opened the door to enter, the increased volume of the music made him cringe. He realized this was all a mistake. He had only come to spend time with Matt, and now here he was standing out front by himself. The weight of isolation intensified. He finally pulled out his phone to send Matt a message, and he saw he had one waiting for him from Eddie. "Good luck tonight," it said with a symbol of a hand with fingers crossed. Then, as he changed message threads to the one with Matt, he received two messages at the same time. One was from Jennifer. It said, "I'm sorry. Please come in." He wondered if she really wanted him to come inside or if she simply realized that he still had their beer. The ambiguity heightened his uncertainty, contemplating the motives behind her gesture. He assumed the latter. The other message was from Matt. His heart skipped a beat, and he felt lightheaded. Realizing he needed to sit down, he walked toward the front steps as he read the message.

"Hey, Will - Jennifer said you left without me. I'll be there soon. Hope you're ok." He was glad to hear from him. He sat down because the lightheadedness he felt a moment ago was nothing compared to what he felt now. He was still sure he was getting his hopes up, but at least Matt wasn't avoiding him anymore. The relief mingled with a persistent uncertainty, creating a tumultuous emotional landscape.

Over at Brian's house, he had gone all out for the first party he'd ever thrown. He had used his fake ID to buy more than enough beer. Despite the rumors and jokes, he still got carded for alcohol. Most of the time. He was playing a special playlist he worked on all week to make sure the vibe of the party stayed upbeat and fun. He had bowls of chips and pretzels around the house. This was not your average high school party. The only problem Eddie saw when he arrived with Ella was that Brian and Pete were the only ones there. The house was conspicuously empty, and the music was playing far too loudly for the four of them. The discordant contrast heightened the sense of isolation, amplifying the awkwardness. Brian realized things were not going to plan, so he turned the music down.

"I'm sorry, guys," he said. "I don't really have a lot of friends to invite, but I thought someone would show."

"Don't be silly," Pete offered.

"Yeah," Eddie chimed in. "Who wants a bunch of strangers around anyway." Ella noticed the way he was trying to make Brian feel better, and she smiled at him. "I see you've got cups and beer, and we have the right number of people for beer pong as well."

Brian smiled at this. "Fine," he said, "But you're on Ella's team. She's terrible."

"I'm not terrible!" she protested. "I'm just... strategic." They all laughed and went to the kitchen table, where Brian began laying out red plastic cups.

While William and Eddie were beginning what would be one of the most important nights of their lives across town, Phillip was starting a night of his own with a few of his less upstanding friends. There was a bong on the table between them and beer cans everywhere. Rock music was playing, and one of the guys in the room was playing the air guitar with a little too much enthusiasm. The pulsating rhythm and animated gestures created an amusing spectacle, injecting a burst of liveliness into the otherwise subdued ambiance of the room.

"Okay," Phillip said. "Time for the good stuff." He opened a prescription pill bottle and poured out four pills that did not look pharmaceutical.

"Is that the new x you were talking about?" one of the boys asked.

"Yup," Phillip confirmed. "Bottoms up." His friends each took one pill and left one in Phillips's palm. They all swallowed the tablets and washed them down with some beer. The one who had been playing air guitar looked a little confused.

"Wait," he said. "Is it okay to mix uppers and downers?" He shook his empty beer can.

"It's too late now," Phillip said, and they all laughed. "Tonight's gonna be wild!" The air guitarist started up again with more vigor than ever.

At Jacob's house, William was still sitting on the front steps. He had taken a beer from his backpack and drank most of it when he heard the door open behind him. The creaking entrance heralded a moment of suspense, the abrupt interruption causing him to turn, his gaze meeting an unexpected arrival.

"I said I was sorry," Jennifer pleaded. "Will you please come in? We're playing cups." William figured he was having more fun by himself out there than he would if he went in, but he couldn't think of an excuse. He could hardly tell Jennifer he was waiting to see if her twin brother had feelings for him.

"I, uh," he started, but he didn't have to think of any excuse after all.

"You need three to play cups," came the voice William had been waiting to hear. The voice that called him Will and turned his knees to Jell-o. He turned his head fast enough to give him whiplash, but he felt fine.

"Let's go then," Jennifer insisted. "They're waiting. We're up next." Matt smiled and met William's eyes. William was sure his gaze was saying, "We'll talk later," and suddenly everything was okay.

Back at Brian's house, Eddie was drinking beer from a plastic cup. He slammed the cup down with a cringe on his face. "Okay," he said hoarsely. "You win." Brian and Pete gave each other a cheesy high five. Pete patted his chest and grunted, further emphasizing their cherished display of friendship.

"What do we win?" he demanded to know.

"Not a rematch," Ella said, and everyone laughed.

"How about a little smoke?" Eddie offered and pulled a small baggie from his pocket. Brian nodded.

"Sounds good to me," he said, and they all went to his back deck. Eddie packed a pipe and offered it to Brian.

"Thank you for hosting tonight," Eddie said as Brian accepted his offer. "I'm sorry more people didn't show up."

"Who says I invited anyone else?" Brian joked as he struck a lighter and drew in a breath of smoke. As he exhaled, his eyes grew wide. "This is some good stuff." Brian passed the pipe to Pete, who took a drag and agreed.

"Wow," he said as he coughed uncontrollably. "Where'd you get it?"

"Not from my guy," Ella pondered as she, too, smoked the pipe. "He never has stuff this good."

"It's from Phillip," Eddie said in barely a whisper. Right away, he wished he said anything else. He was embarrassed that he'd returned to the asshole who had treated him and his friends so badly.

"Oh, Eddie," Ella said, clearly disappointed.

"That jerk from the other day?" Brian asked. "Why would you ever associate with him?"

"Well, it's good stuff," Eddie justified. "You said it yourselves." He could tell he wasn't convincing anyone. "And besides," he added. "He gives me a good deal. This was only fifty bucks." he held out his hand with the baggie in it. He noticed everyone was looking at him funny. That wasn't exactly right. They were all looking at him in a different, funny way. Pete looked confused, adding to the bewildering atmosphere as Eddie grappled with the enigmatic expressions that surrounded him, heightening the sense of disquiet. Ella still looked disappointed, and Brian looked hurt. He was hurt that Eddie would let someone talk down to him and his friends and then go back and give the guy money. The conflicting actions left Eddie with a mix of disappointment and confusion, questioning the dynamics at play in their friendship. Worse than that, Brian knew what Pete and Ella knew, but it was Ella who said it first.

"Eddie, are you serious?" she asked. "That should have been like twenty." Eddie didn't understand at first.

"Dude," Pete said plainly, "he's ripping you off." Eddie had never been more angry in his life.

William, Matt, and Jennifer entered Jacob's house. Unlike Brian's house, his was packed with teens, most from Woolstead Academy, some from St. John's. Suddenly, a thought occurred to William. If he stood next to Matt when they were playing cups, they would have to touch hands when they passed the cup down the line. His heart rate increased. He became lightheaded, but he kept his balance. When they got to the table to play cups, Jennifer planted herself firmly between Matt and William. It would be her hand he grazed as the cup was transferred from him to her. His momentary disappointment was replaced by rationality. As much as he wanted to hold Matt's hand again, he wanted to talk to him even more. Someone at the head of the table counted down, "Three, two, one, go!" William drank his designated portion of the beer from the red plastic cup that was filled halfway up. He passed it to Jennifer, picked up the second cup that was sitting on the table before him, and began to drink from that one. Jennifer took two gulps from the first cup and passed it left to her twin just in time to take the second cup from William.

Having finished his part of the drinking game, all William could do was watch his team to see how fast they could down their shares. The raucous activity intensified, contributing to the lively atmosphere of the gathering. He was watching Matt, who slammed down the first cup and took the second from Jennifer. He finished that beer and stacked the second cup on the first. The team opposite them was still drinking when Matt completed the balancing act; William, Jennifer, and Matt had won.

"We're playing the winners," they heard from behind them, and William realized they were going to play until they lost.

At Brian's house, Eddie had completely lost his temper at the news that Phillip had been taking advantage of him. The revelation fueled a surge of anger, unleashing a torrent of emotions that reverberated through the room.

"That son of a bitch," he was seething. "I can't believe his nerve."

"Don't act so surprised," Ella tried to calm him down. "You said it yourself; he's a rich asshole."

"They're all the same," Brian added. "Always looking out for themselves." Eddie was angry, but he knew what they were saying was not true. It couldn't be.

"They're not all the same," he said through his rage. He wanted to say that William was different, but he knew it would fall on deaf ears.

"Just let it go," Pete said. "Lesson learned."

"I don't think I can do that," Eddie said. "I don't think I can let it go."

"You have to," Ella told him. "Let's just enjoy it and have a good night. Brian was nice enough to host." She looked around to try to remind Eddie not to spoil the evening.

"Fuck that," Eddie said. He was in a daze from his rage. "I'm going to go over there and kick his ass."

"Don't do it," Brian pleaded. "Just let it go."

"Yeah," Ella encouraged. "You can go to my guy from now on."

"Right," Pete agreed. "You never have to see him again." The fact was that all his new friends were right. He might have been given a bad deal, but he had agreed to it. All he could do was learn his lesson and avoid Phillip in the future, which would be easy enough. It was his chance to turn his back on someone who never liked him anyway.

"I don't care," Eddie announced. His mind was made up. "Who's coming?"

"You want us to leave Brian's party to go fight some rich kid?" Pete asked. Eddie's fury increased when he learned none of his friends were going to stand at his side. After all, he thought, they had as much reason to be offended as he did.

"If you go, I won't have a partner for the game anymore," Ella tried to appeal to any sense she could find.

"Let's just enjoy our high," Pete pitched in.

"If you get in trouble, it could come back to me," Brian also tried anything he could to prevent a fight.

"You'll be fine," Eddie said.

Meanwhile, William, Jennifer, and Matt had won three consecutive games of cups and were starting to feel the effects of the alcohol. William was also starting to feel anxious. Teens kept bumping shoulders with him. The music seemed to get louder with every song that played.

Laughter felt amplified in his ears, creating a disorienting sensory cacophony as he navigated the crowded and boisterous ambiance.

Matt must have picked up on William's discomfort because he lost the following game. To William, it didn't just look like he lost. It looked like he had lost on purpose. It was possible that he was just full from beer, but William suspected he had other motives. They congratulated the team that beat them and relinquished their spot to the new challengers.

"You okay, Will?" Matt asked him in as low of a voice as possible. Will. "You seemed ready to get out of here." William was feeling fine now, but he also wanted to take the chance to talk to Matt alone.

"Yeah," William said with the small amount of confidence he could muster. "Wanna go to get some fresh air and smoke a little?"

"Absolutely," Matt said. They got most of the way to the back door when Jennifer noticed.

"William!" she shouted over the commotion of the party. "Are you ok?" He was embarrassed; that was what he was. He gave her a thumbs up, and she returned to cheering for one of the teams playing cups at the table. Out back, Matt and William found a quiet spot and sat on the plush grass. There was enough ambient light that they could barely see.

"Are you doing okay?" Matt asked.

"Yeah. I'm fine now," William confirmed.

"Good," Matt smiled. "We can have just as much fun out here, just the two of us." he looked down when he said the last part.

"That's what I always say," William laughed. "No one listens to me." They both smiled.

"Yeah. I guess parties are overrated," Matt admitted.

"It's all just a competition," William tried to explain, but the alcohol was really kicking in by now, and his thoughts escaped him.

While Matt and William (Will) were enjoying the cool night air and each other's company, Phillip and his cohort of misfits were also starting to feel the effects of the drugs they had taken earlier. The friend playing the air guitar earlier was now playing the invisible air drums along to the music. Suddenly, one of Phillip's other friends turned down the music.

"Do you hear that?" he asked the group.

"What the…" Phillip began but stopped mid-thought. Someone shouted a clear "PHIL!" from out front. The teens in Phillip's bedroom all ran to his window and pulled the curtain back. Staggering in his front yard was Eddie, ready to settle his score.

"That stupid asshole," Phillip said.

"What's going on?" one of his friends asked.

"Who's in the mood for a fight?" Phillip asked.

Back at Jacobs, a teen entered the house from the backyard and made his way through the crowd to where Jennifer was still cheering on the reigning cups team. It was between games, and she was shouting over the music to Jacob next to her while the players arranged cups and poured beer.

"William and me?" she said casually, "We're probably going to make it official soon. He's so shy, but I know he's just dying to ask me to Frida's birthday party." The teen from the backyard whispered something in her ear, and she looked confused, as though she were certain she heard him wrong. He jerked his head toward the back door, indicating she should go and look for herself. She worked her way through the tight group of partiers and opened the back door. Although the music was louder and the light poured outside through the open door, neither Matt nor William noticed Jennifer. They were engaged in the most magical, time-stopping kiss they could ever imagine. The world faded away, leaving only the entwining of their lips in a moment suspended in blissful serenity. William was glad they were sitting on the ground because he would have lost his balance otherwise. He and Matt didn't need to talk about the incident.

When they sat together and looked into each other's eyes, they spoke a thousand words without opening their mouths. The unspoken language conveyed emotions, shared memories, and the promise of an unfolding connection. William understood at once that Matt had been as nervous as he was; that's why he was avoiding him at school. But as soon as they sat out back and Matt looked into William's eyes, he knew they felt the same way. He knew they had experienced the same magical fireworks from a single touching of their hands. They were both ready to feel that again. First, Matt had taken William's (Will's) hand, interlocking their fingers. They floated in the air, just as they had in the lounge a few days prior. The sparks had flown. Both boys' hearts beat in their throats. Matt had kissed William, just a peck on the cheek, really. Then William kissed Matt back. Before they knew it, they were passionately making out while the rest of the world disappeared from their thoughts. In that moment, the yard, the music, and the crowd faded into insignificance, leaving only the intensity of their connection. This perfect moment came crashing down with a crescendo of music and a sliver of light coming from inside Jacob's house. The perfect kiss broke with a shout, a voice the boys recognized at once.

"What the fuck?" Jennifer was in tears. A few classmates had gathered around behind her in the doorway. They were whispering and pointing. A few were taking pictures on their cell phones.

"Jen," Matt started.

"Don't," she said as she walked over to them, becoming increasingly aware the party had basically stopped to observe the spectacle.

"I'm sorry," Matt said, but this time it was William who interrupted him.

"I'm not," he said in a low voice, just more than a whisper. Matt turned and looked at him. Jennifer raised her eyebrows. "I was upfront with you, Jennifer," William went on. "I told you I was gay from the beginning, so I'm not sorry." He knew he had just told the entire audience, mostly his classmates, that he was gay. For the third time, he said, "I'm not sorry. Not for being gay. Not for having a crush on Matt. Not for kissing Matt. I'm not going to let anyone ruin the most perfect, magical moment," but for all his confidence in that moment, the situation was beyond his control. The partiers had all spilled in the backyard. Finally, Jacob joined the crowd to see what had disrupted his party.

"What's going on," he asked, but he could see the scene unfolding. The crowd was on one side of the yard, Jennifer, William, and Matt on the other side. Some of the partiers were watching the videos and pictures they had taken, still hardly believing their eyes. Jennifer was still crying. "It's time for you to go," Jacob said to William. "Now." He had overheard key words spoken in the crowd and pieced together what had happened; only he didn't have the background. All he assumed was that William and

Jennifer were supposed to be together, and she found her would-be date kissing her twin brother. William got to his feet and looked from Jennifer to Matt to Jacob to the crowd and back to Matt. There was no right answer to what to do. He ran. He ran around the house and to his car. It was his father's car that he had taken again, this time with permission, but he was too drunk to drive. He sat in the driver's seat and cried. He was embarrassed. He was angry. He wished Matt had followed him. A tear dropped on the steering wheel, and he was ready to go. He slammed the car into gear and screeched the tires as he peeled out, leaving behind echoes of heartache and the burning rubber of his hurried departure, a visceral manifestation of the emotional turbulence within him.

A few miles away, a different group of teens was gathering in a different yard for a different confrontation. Eddie was enraged when Phillip came outside through the front door. Eddie was ready for a fight, but his confidence lessened with each of Phillip's friends who followed him out. He had never been in a fight before, and here he was, facing four boys, all his size or larger. His rage got the better of him. He balled his right hand into a fist, cocked it back to his shoulder, and thrust it with all his drunken might toward Phillip.

Unfortunately, Phillip easily dodged the punch and shoved Eddie hard. The altercation escalated, each movement laden with the weight of unresolved tensions and the clash of conflicting emotions. Eddie went down, his coordination being compromised from the alcohol. As he tried to get back to his feet, Phillip kicked him in the stomach, and he went back down with a cough.

"Is that all you got?" Phillip taunted. "You come all the way over here and just drop like a baby?"

At the same time, William was driving his father's car home. He felt a buzz in his pocket and pulled out his phone. There was a new message from Leah. She reminded him that their parents were coming home tomorrow and he needed to bring the car back as soon as possible.

"Fuck!" William shouted at the top of his lungs. This wasn't specifically a response to his sister's message but a cathartic release. He tossed the phone on the passenger seat and kept driving. He was almost home now.

Only a few blocks away, Eddie was now being kicked by four teens from all directions. He tried to cover his face with his hands, but his nose and mouth were already bloody. He writhed and tried to crawl across the lawn. His assailants, high on drugs and adrenaline, laughed as they outnumbered Eddie, who never had a chance.

"I never want to see you again," Phillip told him and leaned in to give one last punch to Eddie's gut. He groaned with pain and fell flat on his stomach. Realizing the beating had stopped, he scrambled to his feet and ambled back to the street.

William was crying again, barely able to see the road ahead of him, but he was close to home and sure he could make it. As he turned the corner, he saw someone in his headlights. His tears reminded him of tears from another time a few years in the past. He thought of the time in his bedroom when Eddie told him he was leaving Woolstead. They both cried, and they made a pact always to put their friendship first.

"What are we going to do?" younger Eddie asked younger William, having just shared the news he was transferring to public school

"Well, it's Friday night," younger William said. "I think we should get my brother to get us some beer."

"He's home on break?" younger Eddie asked.

"Yeah," younger William confirmed. "I'll go ask him." He went down the hall to his brother's room and knocked on the door. No answer. He moved on to the lounge, where he found his older brother and older sister smoking marijuana together.

"Oh shit!" his older brother shouted. "Get out of here!" But William didn't move.

"William!" Leah yelled. "Shut the door, for god's sake." William did as she instructed, but he also realized that for the first time in his life, perhaps, he had the upper hand on both his siblings at the same time. He smiled, knowing he was going to get what he wanted.

"I won't tell Mom and Dad," he led with. "But you have to buy some beer for Eddie and me."

"You're too young to drink," his brother protested.

"Just do it so he doesn't tell," Leah argued.

In the present time, William squinted through his tears to see what the object was in front of him. Realizing it was Eddie, he first sped the car up to meet where Eddie was, then he slammed on the brakes, bringing it to a screeching halt. William got out of the car, leaving the door open and the engine running, and he ran to his best friend. He put his arm around Eddie to support him while he helped him back to the car.

"What happened?" he asked his bloodied friend, but Eddie didn't speak. After a few steps, both boys collapsed. They fell onto the pavement in each other's arms and wept.

Bend or Break
Chapter Eleven

The following week, nothing was back to normal, not really. Lingering tension permeated every interaction, casting a shadow over the usual routines as the aftermath of the tumultuous events endured.

Eddie didn't know if he was going to be able to patch things up with Ella, Pete, and Brian after the way he acted and bailed from Brian's party. He hoped his bruised face would elicit some pity, but he didn't count on it.

William and Matt hadn't spoken since Jacob's party. He was avoiding both Matt and Jennifer. What was seemingly back to normal was that Eddie and William were spending time together again. After school one day, they met at the park for their old ritual and then walked back to William's for dinner. Eddie's black eye and slung arm served as reminders of what would be his final interaction with Phillip. Neither he nor William would ever enter that house again, and with Phillip at St. Johns still, William didn't have to worry about running into him at school.

"I can't believe we started our exams today," William began, always the studious one.

"Yeah," Eddie agreed. "I think I drooled on my math bubble sheet."

"Oh well," William said, "At least it's almost Friday."

"We have the whole weekend ahead of us," Eddie smiled. "What are we going to do?"

"I don't know," William said as usual. "You always have good ideas."

After they spent the afternoon at the park, they walked back to William's house. As they walked up the driveway, Eddie nudged William's arm and looked down at the ground, a moment bursting with unspoken thoughts and a shared connection.

"Hey," he said weakly, but he didn't have to finish his thought.

"We can act like it never happened," William comforted his friend.

"Good," Eddie said. "Thanks."

"Just for the record," William added.

"Me too," Eddie smiled. They didn't need to apologize. Their friendship always came first. They entered the front door and were greeted by Lynn.

"Hello, William. Hello, Edward," she said, and then she saw Eddie's face and his arm in a sling. "Edward! What happened?"

"There was a riot in the cafeteria at school," Eddie said with a sideways glance at William and a smile.

"I don't believe it," Lynn said, but of course she did believe it.

"I'm fine," Eddie insisted. "How was your trip?"

"Just lovely," she started as the three walked to the dining room table. Eddie and William shared a secret smile as she turned her back.

Later that night, as the boys lay in bed waiting for sleep but not impatiently, they finally delved into their feelings. They weren't so much explaining to the other - neither owed an explanation - as they were exploring their thoughts through the medium of speech. William lay in his bed, the sheets barely disturbed, his mummy-shaped outline visible through the blanket. The stillness in the room mirrored the quiet turmoil within him, encapsulated by the undisturbed linens and the solitude of his contemplation.

He wore pajamas tonight, which he usually did on nights when he didn't drink and go on adventures until the sun was almost up. His hair was combed back, and his face was clearly illuminated in the sparse light filtering through the gaps in the blinds. The gentle glow accentuated the thoughtful expression etched on his face as he pondered the events unfolding in the recesses of his mind.

Eddie was on the pull-out bed that glided easily from beneath the main structure of the bed. His blankets were a mess, but he was curled up as if feeling cold, and his back was toward William. The disarray of the bedding mirrored the internal disquiet. It would not have mattered if he had been lying on his back or even facing William's direction; the difference in height between the mattresses made it so the boys could not see each other. Even though six days had passed since their party mishaps, both the boys were reliving the events in their heads.

William rolled in bed so he faced Eddie's direction, and he found it easier to begin talking with the visual separation. He knew he would feel a warmth in his ears if he were under Eddie's direct gaze. He was ready to speak, but the words didn't come easily. Every time he thought of what he wanted to say, the words stuck in his throat as if his body was warning him he was about to say the wrong thing. The weight of unspoken thoughts hung heavy in the air, creating a barrier between him and the vulnerability he sought.

Finally, two words managed to slip out in a whisper. "I'm sorry."

"We said we weren't going to apologize," Eddie said, also whispering.

"But I am," William dared to confirm, "for so much. I'm sorry I chose Phillip because he was convenient. I'm sorry I fell for the first jerk who ever paid me any attention."

"Stop," Eddie bade, "because I'm sorry too. Anyone could see Jennifer was still into you. I should have said something that day…" but he trailed off as he realized what William had said about Matt. They hadn't discussed him since William was head over heels, so hearing William call Matt a jerk was surprising, although not a sentiment Eddie disagreed with. "What do you mean he's a jerk?" Eddie asked. His pupils dilated as he asked the question, and under the blanket, his hands tensed in anticipation of William's response. The room held its breath, the unarticulated query hanging between them.

"He should have had my back at the party," William started, although he hadn't fully worked through his thoughts before he spoke them. "I touched his hand and thought I fell in love, but he's really just like Jennifer when you think about it."

"I thought you liked Jennifer," Eddie said, "up until the party, I mean."

"I did," William explained, speaking in just above a whisper now. "But when I look back, I missed all the signs." Eddie knew William would go on and didn't say a word. "She was fake, always with the flattery. And I know she had to have known something happened between Matt and me. Since we touched hands, I thought he was avoiding me, but she was making excuses to exclude him. Then, at the party, they both showed their true selves. She turned everyone against me, and he turned into a mute." The divulgence unraveled the tangled web of misunderstandings, shedding light on the intricate dynamics at play within their social circle.

"Coward," Eddie said in agreement, but he closed his eyes and exhaled through his nose, knowing he was describing himself as much as Matt with this single word. He was almost ready to relieve himself of the proverbial scarlet letter (or at least trade it for a new one), but he wasn't quite ready yet.

"I was a little bit jealous, too, to tell the truth," William continued. It didn't even occur to Eddie that William meant he was jealous of him. He assumed he was jealous of Matt for some twisted reason. "I was jealous that you started your new job and made all these new friends. You know I've always wanted to have our own little clique, and I felt like you went off, and I was left out." William almost laughed. "It sounds so stupid when I say it out loud, but…" he didn't know the ending to the thought he started to say it aloud.

"But you're right," Eddie admitted. "I was jealous, too. Of you and Matt and Jennifer. I thought you were having fun without me, and I'm sorry." He was done with the surface-level apologies and after-the-fact analysis.

Their friendship was deeper than this. But Eddie closed his eyes again, disappointed in himself and thinking back to the word coward. Their friendship would never be as deep as they thought as long as he held this secret. He thought back to the night the boys had been in the exact same spots, William in bed and him on the pull-out. He had asked William what was wrong, and he had mustered the courage to admit his truth. He took a leap of faith that his best friend wouldn't judge him, and he was right. As long as Eddie didn't have the same faith in William, their perfect friendship was really marred. He had tried to tell William twice before. Once casually, which didn't work at all, he lost his nerve immediately and abandoned the plan.

The second time, he had come close, but he didn't know quite what to say. After all, he hadn't truly discovered the label that applied to his sexuality. Was he gay? Was he bisexual? He didn't know, and he used that as an excuse not to tell William. He couldn't hide behind that any longer. His friendship had been rocky for a few weeks, and then it boomeranged back to its old brilliance. The ebbs and flows had forged a resilient bond, weathering the storm and emerging stronger than before. Now was the time for grand gestures of trust, not simple apologies and summarizing of transgressions.

"I have to tell you something," Eddie said, back to a whisper.

"Okay," William matched his tone and volume. Eddie hesitated.

"Don't let me not tell you," Eddie went on slowly, imagining the confused expression on William's face. "Because I might try to back out and not tell you." Now, his face was twisted with confusion by his own convoluted words. He was talking in circles.

"You're not going to tell me you're gay?" William said and laughed. Eddie didn't laugh. His eyes widened so that the entire grey irises could be seen if the lights had been bright enough in the bedroom. In all the ways he had played through this scenario, nothing like this had ever happened. He froze, having no idea how to respond. He tried to collect his thoughts, and at the same time, William realized an eternity had passed since he made his joke, and Eddie neither responded nor laughed. The reality of what he had done sank in. Another eternity passed, and finally, Eddie found his voice.

"I'm," was all he needed to say for William to get the confirmation he needed. He gasped. He wasn't simply surprised. He audibly gasped and clapped his hand over his mouth to try to hide it. The unexpected revelation elicited a visceral reaction, shattering the facade of composure and laying bare the depth of his astonishment. It was too late, but it was also the perfectly comical reaction the moment needed. Both boys laughed at William's reaction to the news that, in reality, had not yet been delivered. "I'm," Eddie repeated, finding his confidence in his friendship. "Not sure if I'm gay or bi. I kept saying to myself that I would tell you as soon as I knew which, but you deserve to know."

"I don't deserve to know," William corrected. "And I'm glad you didn't tell me before you were ready. This is big news. I need to let it sink in. Let's get some sleep, and we'll celebrate by getting some rainbow flags first thing in the morning." Eddie knew William was joking, but he needed to say one or two more things before they each pretended to sleep. On second thought, William did have one question. "What about Ella?" he asked. "Did you really have feelings for her?"

"That's the thing," Eddie began. He had asked himself the same question for the past several days. When Ella told him that she wanted to go to Brian's party just as friends, that she wasn't sure she wanted to be in a relationship, Eddie had felt relief, not disappointment. "I think I was just caught up in things." He tried to explain. "We had been spending so much time together at work and school, and you were talking about having feelings for someone. It just felt like what I was supposed to do. I don't know if that makes sense."

"More than you know."

"I'm glad I told you," was the next thing Eddie needed to say. It was true. He felt a weight lifted off his chest, and he breathed easier than he had since he could remember. "Can we keep this just between us for now while I'm figuring things out?" he asked.

"Of course," William said. This was hardly the biggest secret either was keeping for the other. Eddie had a final thing on his mind.

"I'm glad you realized Matt was a jerk," he said with a small cringe. He wasn't sure how William would take it, but he laughed.

"Why didn't you tell me?" William asked, but there was no answer. Eddie wasn't sure if he was asking why he hadn't told him Matt was a jerk or why he hadn't told him he wasn't straight. As William rolled over and the boys lay back-to-back on separate beds, both thought of how their friendship would change because of the news. William was excited to be included in such a personal part of Eddie's life and knew it would bring them closer. The prospect ignited a spark of anticipation, fostering the promise of strengthened bonds and a deeper connection. Eddie was thinking of their friendship changing in another way. He was discovering that he had feelings for his best friend. It was scary and exciting at the same time. Neither would sleep much that night.

The next morning, Eddie was gathering his things while William was down the hall. As Eddie checked his pockets for his keys, phone, and wallet, he grabbed two energy drinks from the mini fridge under the desk, one for him and one for the soon-to-be returning William. As he heard a noise at the door, he turned and tossed the can toward whom he expected to be William. It was Leah. She caught the can without flinching, opened the can, and drank a hearty swig.

"Hey there," she said in her deadpan way. "Haven't seen you around lately." She, like her father, was not one to use four words when three would suffice.

"No," Eddie agreed and admitted. "I guess I've been working." He trailed off.

"You've been working," Leah repeated. "I see." She took another gulp of the energy drink.

"Yeah. At the Taco Plaza," Eddie continued.

"Oh, I know," Leah said. "William told us all about it." There was a long moment of silence, and Eddie wished she would either fill it or continue down the hallway, preferably the latter. The weight of the unstated lingered uncomfortably.

She chose the former. "Before William told us about your job, I thought maybe you'd found a girlfriend, and that's why you weren't around."

"A girlfriend," Eddie repeated and nervously laughed. "Not me."

"No, of course not," Leah began. What did she mean by that, Eddie wondered? Had she been listening in on their conversation the night before? What was she implying? "Because William told me you two ruined each other for dating." She blinked at Eddie and stared directly into his eyes. She heard William returning and decided it was time to stop messing with Eddie. "Anyway," she said. "Nice catching up." She threw the can back at him. He flinched, expecting it to be half-full of liquid and to splash onto him. Instead, the empty can meet his stomach with a much over-exaggerated reaction. He fumbled with the can as William returned to the room. Luckily, Eddie got ahold of it before it could do any real damage and without embarrassing himself too badly.

Bend or Break
Chapter Twelve

The next day held surprises in store for William and Eddie. It would be a stretch to say nothing went as planned because neither of them really had a plan.

At school, William noticed he was getting more attention than usual. A few weeks ago, that level of attention would have been zero. After Jacob's party, he got a few stares and whispers, but today, it seemed like everyone was pointing at him. The collective attention intensified, casting a spotlight on him, making the stares and whispers feel magnified and inescapable. He looked down to confirm he was wearing pants and hadn't shown up for school in his underwear. What was everyone looking at? He went to his locker and made it to class without seeing Matt or Jennifer, which was fine with him. He was in no rush to see either of them. Classes were over for the year, and only exams were left. William's first exam was physics, and it was in the form of a practical exam, meaning the students would work in pairs to conduct some sort of experiment to demonstrate the lessons taught during the previous months. William's lab partner was Nathan Woo. They didn't really know each other before taking this class, but they sat next to each other on the first day and were thereafter designated as lab partners for the year. The chance seating arrangement blossomed into a year-long partnership, weaving the threads of connection through shared academic endeavors.

William went to the store room to gather the supplies he and Nathan would need: a bunsen burner, a test tube, tongs, and, of course, gloves and goggles.

As he left the storeroom and re-entered the classroom, he saw a few of the popular boys giving Nathan a hard time. When they saw William, they quickly went back to their lab tables and pretended to mind their own business.

"What was that all about?" William asked as he handed Nathan his gloves and goggles. Although they had basically started the year as strangers, they had formed a cordial relationship since September.

"Nothing," Nathan said coldly. "Let's just get this done."

"What's going on today?" William asked, genuinely confused. "I feel like everyone is acting so strange." Nathan was not confrontational, but he was curious. He hadn't been invited to Jacob's party, but he heard about the infamous kiss the following Monday at school. What he just learned was the latest development that could turn much of the school against William, at least for now.

"I have calc with Matt," Nathan said in a low voice as he put the goggles on his face and stretched the elastic band around his head.

"I don't want to talk about him," William said, but he didn't realize that Nathan was trying to deliver the news he had waited all morning to hear. He was trying to explain why everyone was looking at William like he'd left his pants at home.

"But that's the thing," Nathan went on, knowing William would want him to ignore the protests. "He's talking about you."

"What do you mean?" William asked as he tried to tie his rubber apron behind his back. Suddenly, his fingers didn't work, and his head was full of bubbly water. He was getting dizzy, and his vision was fading. Luckily, his stool was directly behind him, or he might have fallen backward onto his bottom on the floor.

"I don't want to get in the middle of anything," Nathan hesitated, but it was too late. He had started a story he now had to finish.

"You're not," William insisted. "Just tell me what he said."

"He said you got him drunk," Nathan, who had until then met William's eyeline, blurted out as he looked down. "He said you got him drunk and tried to kiss him." William was beet red. How could Matt say this? How could anyone believe it? There was a party full of witnesses who had seen them both playing cups and smoking marijuana together in the backyard and even more who had seen them kissing, consensually kissing. It had even been recorded on more than one cell phone. He thought about asking to go to the nurse, but he knew not to bother during the exam period. He continued with the lab and got to thinking about how to handle Matt's situation.

Eddie had taken the previous several days off work to prepare for exams. He had guaranteed his mother that his grades wouldn't slip as a result of the new job, and if he was honest, they didn't have much room to slip anyway this semester. Today was his first shift in five days. It was his first shift since Brian's party. He was in jeopardy of seeing Pete, Brian, Ella, or all three. He had sent an apology text to the group after he embarrassed himself at the party, but he never heard back. Ever since his renewed friendship with William, he didn't really care. Before he had the chance to see whom he was working with, he was confronted by the manager when he went to the back room to put on his apron and hat to complete his uniform.

"Eddie," the manager said. "Can I see you a moment?" Eddie went into the small office and closed the door behind him. "Get into a fight?" the manager asked and used a pen to point to Eddie's black eye and arm, but he didn't let Eddie answer. "You're new, so I'm going to cut you a break, but if you come in with a black eye again, you're going home. Understand?"

"Yes, sir," Eddie said respectfully, but he was struggling not to roll his eyes.

"I would put you on prep, but I imagine you can't do much with that arm," the manager said. "I guess you'll have to be on the cash register with Ella tonight." Eddie flinched at the sound of Ella's name. The last thing he wanted to do was spend the evening with her. Between the crush that neither of them really had for the other and his embarrassment over his behavior at Brian's party, he didn't even know where to begin. He had to remind himself he was not spending the evening with her. This was not a social call; it was work, and Eddie hoped it would be busy. He thought of Ella awkwardly looking at him, waiting for an explanation or an apology. He had neither to offer, and she didn't expect them after all. She'd gotten an apology text, and even with Phillip at St. John's, word had spread to Grissom (and Woolstead, for that matter) about the fight. No, she didn't expect an explanation or an apology from Eddie.

When he got to the register where he would spend the next several hours, Ella was already at hers. She chose the register all the way to one end of the counter, presumably so Eddie could work from the opposite end. He knew this was protocol so the line would flow better when they were busy, but it felt intentional on Ella's part. Eddie was just accustomed to his training shifts when he would work right next to her, and he knew he was being silly. He reminded himself again this wasn't a social visit. He gave her a halfhearted smile and a little wave from his end of the counter. He clocked in and greeted the next customer in line, seamlessly transitioning into the routine of the workday.

With his once-again only friend at work for the evening and only one exam remaining for William, he found himself restless. He put on some music, but that didn't hold his attention. He played a video game but got bored after ten minutes. He scrolled through social media, first looking up the pages for the college he wanted to attend, but he was quickly sidetracked into looking at Jennifer's page. He then tried to look at Matt's against his better judgment, but he couldn't find Matt's page.

The only explanation was that Matt had blocked him, which he supposed made sense after the morning's news from Nathan Woo. William was thinking about transferring to St. John's like Phillip had. Could he run from his problems? He was convincing himself he could when a figure appeared in his doorway. It was Leah, in her pajamas, holding up two spoons. "You know what we haven't done in ages?" She asked rhetorically. William smiled even though Leah reminded him of an older sibling being forced to include a younger brother. Maybe she was bored tonight, too. Whatever the reason, he was happy for the distraction. "Ice cream and gossip," she confirmed.

They went downstairs to the kitchen and took a few coffee mugs from the cupboard. It was a family oddity to eat ice cream from mugs rather than bowls. They retrieved their favorite flavors from the freezer: chocolate for Leah and coffee for William. He took a few big scoops for himself and handed the scooper to his sister, who did the same. They both topped their mugs with whipped cream from a can and sat side by side at the breakfast bar on raised stools. Leah ate a bite of her chocolate ice cream with whipped cream and held the spoon up to her mouth like a microphone, adding a playful touch to their shared moment.

"I'm here live with William Blake," she said, mimicking the tone of a news reporter. "So tell us, William. What *is* the gossip?" William took a bite of pure whipped cream and smiled.

"You are such a dork," he proclaimed and nudged her shoulder with his, but the grin on his face revealed the truth that he was loving this farce. It had been a year or more since the two siblings had played this game. They called it

Ice Cream and Gossip, but Ice Cream Confessional would have been just as apt a name. They ate too much ice cream (usually two rounds, sometimes three if the conversation was good enough) and told one another about the things going on in their life. Difficult things, ordinary things, it didn't matter. Even though William was smiling, this round of Ice Cream and Gossip got serious pretty quickly. The lighthearted atmosphere took a sharp turn, and an undercurrent of seriousness permeated their conversation, reshaping the dynamic.

"I guess you heard," William said, hoping he wouldn't have to tell the story from the beginning.

"I heard a rumor," Leah confirmed. This was a relief. William thought for a moment that he wouldn't have to tell her directly until she continued, "But I don't listen to rumors, you know me. Only you know what really happened."

"That's not exactly true," William correctly pointed out. "I wasn't the only one there." He realized he would have to tell the story from the beginning. It started with Jennifer and Matt coming over that day with Danny. He told Leah about coming out to Jennifer in the park, her asking him a series of questions about it, and how she continued to pursue him after that. He told her of the incident with the pool cue and touching Matt's hand. She smiled and rolled her eyes at this. Young love was so innocent. But his story shifted from love to hate as soon as he got to the part where Matt sold him out at the party and started a rumor that William got him drunk and took advantage of him.

"I wonder if Danny knows," Leah pondered. He thought it was interesting that was her first reaction.

"That his little brother's gay?" William asked.

"No. Who cares about that," Leah said flatly. "I wonder if he knows about the rumor Matt started."

"Why would he care?"

"He's a good guy," Leah explained. "Regardless of what you think of him, he would not be ok with Matt doing that to you."

"What if he doesn't know it's a lie?" William asked, adding a slight complication to the matter.

"He will soon," Leah confirmed. William was a bit overwhelmed. Just an hour earlier, in his bedroom, he was feeling more alone than he actually was. Suddenly, he had someone on his side. Even if Nathan Woo had believed him when he told him the rumor was false, that wasn't going to get him very far.

Having Leah stand with him gave him a new confidence. The simple act of companionship created a subtle but profound shift, empowering him with a newfound assurance that radiated in his demeanor. The idea that Danny might help with the situation gave him even more hope. To William, the term 'the situation' no longer referred to a brief and accidental touching of hands; it referred to an intentional lie, an act of malice that required another act to balance it out. This alliance of Leah, Eddie, and perhaps Danny gave him hope that balance was possible. It certainly was not while he stood alone. The collective support hinted at the potential for equilibrium in his life, a reassurance that together they could navigate challenges.

This wasn't exactly how the game of Ice Cream and Gossip was supposed to go. It was usually lighter, and at the same time, William wanted to shift the attention to his older sister. He knew there was one more confession he needed to confess.

"I," he began and cleared his throat to speak with confidence. "I don't like girls." Sometimes, it was easier to say it this way than to say he was gay. Anyway, now it was out in the open, and all he could do was wait for her reaction. She lifted her spoon to her lips like a microphone again and turned to her brother.

"That hasn't been good gossip in about a decade," she said in her fake reporter's voice. They both laughed. What else could they do? William nudged her with his shoulder as they sat side by side, eating their ice cream.

"Well, Leah Blake," he said in his version of a newscaster. "What is the gossip?" She took another bite of her ice cream and thought for a moment.

"Things are getting pretty serious with Danny," she said in a more serious tone.

"Gross," William said as they both laughed.

"Not like that," she insisted. "I really like him. And we're both going to Cornell in the fall, so if things work out…"

"That's really great," William said, and he was actually happy for her.

"I'm going to talk to him tomorrow, and we'll see what we can do about your Bill Cosby situation."

"Don't even joke," William said, but they were both howling by now. How they could be laughing about something so terrible and something that was ruining William's reputation (let alone possibly get him arrested if it were true), they didn't know, but they were laughing. At that moment, everything was good.

Chapter Thirteen

Leah was eager to talk to Danny and get his take on the rumor his little brother had been spreading. Normally, and despite the session of Ice Cream and Gossip that evening, she could not have been less concerned with rumors and gossip. This would have been especially true regarding a few boys two years younger than Leah and all her friends. However, when it came to family, she had a protective instinct. She didn't know if it was a maternal thing or an older sister thing, but she did not tolerate her little brother being picked on or bullied. Her protective instincts flared, and she stood as an unwavering shield against any injustice directed at him, fostering a formidable sisterly defense. This was worse.

She remembered back to the time before Eddie moved into the neighborhood and became friends with William. She remembered how William was always ostracized by his peers and excluded from games. She would include him in the games of the older students at the risk of being judged by her own classmates. She remembered the first birthday of William's after Eddie was in the picture.

Bend or Break

William had invited about twenty-five friends to the bowling alley, and Eddie was the only one who actually showed up. He found out later that a more popular girl was throwing her own birthday party at the same time. Not only had she neglected to tell him, but none of the other students had either, and they chose to attend her birthday party instead.

Leah made sure that William and Eddie had a great time at the bowling alley, and even though the only ones singing Happy Birthday were family and Eddie (he was family, too, wasn't he, even back then?), it was one of the best birthdays William could remember. That was the power of a big sister, and Leah used her power for good. At least most of the time.

After she and William finished their ice cream - only one round tonight - the siblings went back to their respective bedrooms. Leah texted Danny to ask if he would drive her to school tomorrow. She was glad when he texted right back that he would. Not only did this give them the opportunity to talk about Matt, but she also felt they were getting closer all the time. It was probably just puppy love, she cautioned herself, but she also really liked him.

William felt more encouraged after their talk. The ice cream helped, too. In his room, he turned on some music and tried not to stress about the situation.

In reality, there was only a week left of exams, and then school would be out for the summer. Surely, he could make it through another week, especially since he only had to show up for his single remaining exam. He tried to think of what his life would be like a week later when he was off for the summer. He and Eddie would make the most of their time, even if Eddie was going to be working at the Taco Plaza.

When Danny pulled into the driveway, Leah darted out the front door and got in his car, a newer model Volkswagen sedan. She gave him a peck on the cheek, and they said good morning to each other.

"Is William coming?" he asked. The fact that he even asked set off a chain reaction of thoughts in Leah's head. The thoughts all basically boiled down to the same conclusion: If Danny was on Matt's side of things, he would not have wanted William to come along. But what if he was just being nice to his soon-to-be girlfriend? She suddenly became aware that too much time had passed since he asked his question.

"He doesn't have an exam this morning," was all Leah could come up with. She actually didn't know if he did or not, but she did know that she couldn't have the conversation that needed to be had with William in the back seat.

"Ok," Danny said and shifted the car into reverse. "You have world history this morning?" he asked, but he knew the answer. He had been helping her study, and this was the one she was worried about. Ever since talking to William the night before, she hadn't thought about the exam once.

"I need to ask you something," she said, ignoring his question. "And normally it would be none of my business, but." She didn't finish her sentence.

"I haven't even talked to Meghan in weeks," he said a little bit defensively.

"No, not that," Leah laughed. They weren't dating (although they had been on several dates), and she was not the jealous type. His response was sweet, though. "It actually has to do with our brothers." She hoped he knew what she was alluding to, but he didn't.

"I haven't heard anything," Danny said, "but I haven't seen William around. Did they get into some sort of a fight or something?"

"Not exactly," Leah began to explain. "It's a little bit delicate, so I don't want to catch you off guard."

"Just tell me," he urged and took her left hand in his right. "It's okay."

"There's a rumor going around Woolstead that Matt started," she continued, but she knew she needed to give a little more context. "There was a party last week at one of the second-year's houses, and William and Matt were there along with Jennifer. Apparently, Jennifer and a bunch of the other kids saw Matt and William kissing in the backyard." She waited for this news to sink in. She knew she might have been outing his little brother, and how would he react if she were? Would he deny that his younger brother had been kissing another boy? Would he become angry at the accusation? She thought about making an excuse for the kiss. A lot of boys experiment; it doesn't mean he's gay, is what she thought to say, but it didn't feel right. Her brother wasn't simply experimenting and finding himself, and she doubted Matt was either.

"So what does this have to do with us?" That was all Danny asked. "If Matt wants to go around kissing boys, that's fine with me, but why tell me about it now?"

"Well," she was surprised at how aloofly he was taking this news. Had Matt come out to him already? Had they already discussed it? Maybe he really just didn't care one way or the other. "Like I said, there's a rumor going around that Matt started."

"Tell me."

"He's saying William got him drunk intentionally to take advantage of him." She said and waited for the words to make their way from her lips, through his ears, to his brain. It took less than a second because she saw his eyes widen.

"I'll talk to him tonight," Danny said resolutely. "Leave it to me. He will make this right."

At the same time the students at Woolstead Academy were preparing for their morning exams, their counterparts at Grissom High School were doing the same thing. The parallel scenes unfolded with an uncanny synchronicity, bridging the geographical and economical gap between the two schools and emphasizing the shared rhythm of academic endeavors. Eddie was as lucky as William to have the morning off, so he slept in before reviewing his notes one last time ahead of his Geometry exam. He flipped through the notes and decided to go to William's house. He walked the distance in less than twenty minutes and knocked on the door. He didn't know if William's mother was home or if she was out somewhere, being active in the community this morning.

After a beat, William answered the door and led the way to the lounge room. If his father were home, they would have gone out back or up to William's bedroom. William shut the door to the lounge behind them, which was unusual.

The next thing Eddie knew, William's arms were around him, and their lips were pressed together in more of a smoosh than a kiss. They blinked and closed their eyes. William ran his hand through Eddie's curly hair and left his hand caressing the back of Eddie's head as he tilted his own head for a real kiss. Eddie couldn't breathe. He knew what it must be like for someone allergic to bees to get stung and have their throat close up, although he was experiencing none of the pain of a bee sting.

As he tried to find his breath, the walls fell around them, and they were floating in mid-air. Then the sky itself collapsed, and they were in the vacuum of space where breath didn't matter anyway. The surreal sequence unfolded, transcending the confines of reality and plunging them into a cosmic dreamscape. They were a million miles from the earth. William's hand in his hair was like a bolt of lightning to his heart. He tried again to breathe and found his body was not responding to requests from his brain. Only his lips were aware of themselves, but they were listening to his heart, not his brain. This was Eddie's first kiss, and he finally understood what all the hype was about. This was magic, and he was going to get as much as he could.

After what seemed like an hour or maybe two seconds, their lips parted, but they remained in a tight embrace. "Eddie," William whispered softly. Dale Carnegie wrote that a person's name is the sweetest sound in any language (or something close to that), and Eddie thought he was wrong. He knew now that it depended on who said it. Surely, it wasn't sweet when his mother called his name to reprimand him for his grades, but when William said it, it was *sweet*. Sweet and warming. What was there to say?

"William," he started, hoping the sound of his name would evoke the same feelings of sweetness and warmth. "It was always you." He was glad they were still hugging because a tear fell from his eye, grazed his cheek, and landed on William's shoulder with a tiny splash. However, instead of silently absorbing into William's shirt, the tear landed with a deafening BUZZ, and suddenly, Eddie was alone in his own bed.

"A dream?" he whispered to himself, tugging on his shirt, which clung to his chest from sweat. He hit the snooze button on his alarm and looked at the clock. It was after ten o'clock. He had really slept in, and he was too distracted by his dream to think about his exam that afternoon. He turned off the alarm, stood up, and checked his phone. Standing in his plaid flannel pants and his shirt still clinging to his damp chest, he saw he had a message from William. He almost dropped his phone as he stubbed his toe hard on the dresser. Simultaneously, he felt the throbbing pain in his foot and a very different pounding in his chest.

"Good luck with your exam. Come over after." That was all the message said. Eddie responded with a symbol of a hand, giving a thumbs-up gesture. Suddenly, he was nervous and not at all for his exam.

William spent the next five hours as he had planned. He reviewed his notes and studied for his test. He walked to school and glided right through his exam. He didn't run into Jennifer or Matt, and the rest of the students seemed to have already begun forgetting the gossip that plagued him recently. He was once again invisible among the swarms of teens, and he enjoyed his crowded solitude. The anonymity within the bustling crowd provided a sense of comfort, a peaceful blend of being surrounded by others yet immersed in his personal thoughts.

The rush of students at each bell between classes always reminded William of being in a big city. He had been to New York a few times, and Chicago once with his dad, and his favorite part was the crowds. He usually didn't like to be among people, but in the city, you could be invisible. You could be alone among the masses. The urban anonymity offered solace, allowing one to navigate the vibrant crowd while remaining cocooned in personal contemplation.

Those same five hours skipped by for Eddie as though he had slept through them. He couldn't remember getting ready to go to school. He couldn't recall if he had done any last-minute studying. If he did, it didn't matter or do any good. His mind was only engaged in one thought. The walk to school may as well not have happened; he might have crossed the street against oncoming traffic for all he knew. Then there was the exam. It was over as soon as it began.

"Pencils down!" the proctor yelled, and all the teachers monitoring the students paid close attention to ensure no one continued answering questions past the timer. Eddie looked down and saw he had neatly filled in a bubble for each answer, but he couldn't have told one question from the test if his passing grade had depended on it. His mind was a million miles away.

More precisely, it was about two miles away from where he currently sat; it was back in the lounge at William's house. The exam was over, and it was time to head towards his best friend's house. He had never been so nervous in his life. Not on his first day of school at Woolstead or Grissom, not when he interviewed at the Taco Plaza, and not when he drunkenly challenged Phillip to a fight. He had a bonafide crush on his best friend, and he didn't know how to react.

Quite literally, he had not had enough time to process his emotions to know how to respond and how to accept what he was feeling. The whirlwind left him grappling with a complex internal landscape, seeking clarity in the midst of uncertainty. What he knew was that he was not going to be able to hide his confused feelings from William. He was right about that.

William had finished his exam and was ready to start the walk home, but first, he needed to stop by his locker. He had meant to clean it out the day before, but with everyone staring at him in the hallway, he didn't want to spend any more time there than he needed to.

With exams winding down, many students were done for the semester (and year) and had already eagerly emptied their lockers. William was glad for the solitude. He put the few items remaining in the locker into his leather bag. When he closed the locker, his solitude was broken. Just as he closed it, Matt turned the corner and was not standing about thirty feet away.

More importantly, he was standing between William and the exit. William fantasized for a quick moment that Matt hadn't been seeking him out and that this was an accidental encounter, but he couldn't fool himself very long. He felt like a brick landed on his chest. He felt like he was sinking into the ground, and his feet couldn't have moved even if he could have turned and run the other way. His feet seemed incapable of movement, rendering escape impossible. The physical sensations mirrored the emotional burden that enveloped him, a visceral manifestation of the overwhelming impact. He dropped his bag to the ground. He knew there was no avoiding what was coming next. Matt walked slowly toward him.

"Will," he said, almost shouting to get his attention as though it weren't obvious that William had seen him the second he turned the corner. It sickened William that he was reminded of Eddie's go-to joke where he yelled William's name and pretended to get his attention. That was a special joke between the two of them, and Matt was unknowingly ruining it. "Will. We need to talk." As Matt spanned the remaining distance between the two boys, William found his voice.

"Don't call me that," was the first thing that came out of his mouth. "My name is William."

"Sorry," Matt said, as if abbreviating William's name was the only thing he had to be sorry about. The list in William's head was long, but he wasn't interested in apologies. He was ready to move on with his life. "William, I'm sorry." Matt sounded genuine, but he had proven himself a liar. He was cunning, and he could have found a way to explain himself without hurting William. The realization deepened the sense of betrayal, highlighting the deliberate choice to inflict pain in lieu of transparency. For that matter, he could have owned his actions and been himself.

"I don't need an apology," William asserted. "I'm over it, and school's out for the summer. By the time we're back in the fall, no one will remember anyway."

"Danny made me realize how wrong it was," Matt continued. "He knows I'm gay now, thanks to all this. I'm not ready for everyone to know…" William had heard enough.

"He made you realize how wrong it was?" he asked, exasperated. "You didn't know already? You couldn't figure out for yourself that starting that rumor could have ruined me?"

"I know now," Matt insisted, but he missed the point.

"And you think coming out to your brother makes up for what happened?" William asked. "I don't care if you're out or straight or whatever you are, but I know you're not stupid. You kissed me at a party full of people; you had to know someone was going to see."

"I was drunk," Matt said and looked at the floor. This was too close to you got me drunk for William.

"Don't," William cautioned him, then his tone turned gentler. "Look. You take your time and figure things out. No judgment from me, but I can't be a part of it. I'm done, Matt."

The brick was lifted from his chest, and he could breathe again. He heard what he needed to hear, and he said what needed to be said. The exchange marked a turning point, fostering a sense of closure and allowing the weight of unspoken truths to dissipate.

There was nothing left to do but leave. He picked up his bag, slung the strap over his shoulder, and walked past Matt, who stayed in place, looking at the space where William had just stood.

Chapter Fourteen

The fresh air of the afternoon breeze was restorative for William as he walked home. He had envisioned a million ways the interaction with Matt could unfold, and none of those imaginary scenarios came close to how perfectly he felt he handled things. A newfound confidence surged within him, one that wouldn't be broken any time soon. The resilience emanating from within signaled a transformative shift, promising endurance in the face of challenges and an unyielding determination to navigate the path ahead.

When he got home, William went to the lounge to check if Eddie had finished his exam first and beaten him there. To his surprise, no sign of Eddie. William then went to his bedroom and changed from his school uniform into more comfortable clothes. The familiar ritual marked the transition from the structured world of academia to the relaxed sanctuary of his personal space.

Today, he wore blue chinos and a red polo shirt. It felt great to be rid of the tie and blazer, even though he had only worn it through a short afternoon exam. As he ran his fingers through his hair, he heard the door downstairs. It was either Leah or Eddie; there was no way to tell. He grabbed the red pencil case from his school bag and headed down to check. It turned out to be Leah who had arrived first, and she wanted an update. No farce of ice cream and spoon microphones today.

"Danny said he talked to Matt," she said, getting right to the matter at hand. William was glad because he didn't want to discuss it in front of Eddie. As far as he was concerned, Matt was dead to him, and this would be the last time he would discuss the matter. Time would tell if he could make that happen, will it to happen.

"He came to talk to me after the exam," William said, which wasn't much of an explanation.

"Well?" Leah asked. She was in that mother-bear protective-sister mode again.

"Well, nothing," William responded. "He gave me some BS apology. I told him to go to hell, and I'm over it."

"What about the rumors?" she asked.

"Rumor of the week," he said. "I think people are already over it. By the time we're back in the fall, it'll be old news."

"Maybe we can get him kicked out of Woolstead on an honor violation?" Leah posed.

"Nothing happened at school," William refuted, "and besides, I just want to be over it." as the conversation was winding down, Eddie entered through the front door. William widened his eyes and gave Leah a glare that she knew meant they were done talking about Matt.

"Hi William, hi Leah," Eddie said as he came in without knocking. Then, with a big smile, he announced. "School. Is. OUT!" The three of them gave a cheer. Leah felt a bit immature, but she only had one more last day of high school after this, so why not get caught up in the moment?

"Want to celebrate?" William asked as he held up his red pencil case. Eddie smiled, and Leah rolled her eyes.

"What am I fifteen years old?" she joked. She hadn't smoked in a few years, and she might have considered it, but she had other plans. "Danny is coming to pick me up. There's a party for upcoming fourth years at the tree line. No third years." This was good news to Eddie. He knew it would be better with William and him and the elephant in the room. If Leah were there, would he be forced to make his confession more publicly? Even she would likely pick up on his awkwardness. She disappeared into the kitchen while the boys went to William's room.

As they walked up the stairs, William began to feel that Eddie was tentative and quiet since his celebratory outburst. They entered the lounge, and William closed the door behind them. The hushed atmosphere heightened the sense of intimacy, setting the stage for a potentially significant conversation. His intention was to prevent their marijuana smoke from drifting throughout the house, but it gave Eddie a flashback to his dream, and his heart skipped a beat.

"What's up with you?" William asked. "Not feeling great about the exam? It's over now, so all you can do is wait."

"It's not that," Eddie said. "I need to tell you something."

"You already came out," William joked, "don't you remember?" They both laughed, and it was just like old times, with no tension between them. But it wasn't old times, and Eddie needed to say what was on his mind. Strike that; he needed to say what was on his heart.

"I really like you," he said in a low, calm tone.

A big grin crept over William's face, but still looked a little confused, like a child told to choose a puppy from among all those in the litter. Eddie swallowed hard before he continued. "I don't think I'm ready for a boyfriend." was the next set of words to escape his lips. "I don't know what I'm ready for, but I want us to go on a date on Saturday."

William's smile grew bigger; then he bit his lips to try to hide his excitement. He felt dizzy and wondered for a moment if he was dreaming. He meant to say yes, but for a moment, his sardonic head overtook his romantic heart.

"Saturday's tomorrow," he said and laughed through a huge smile. They both laughed.

"That's what I said," Eddie corrected himself, and they both laughed. No, things were not back to usual. They never could be now, but for the moment, they were better than ever. "So, is that a 'yes?'" he asked. William didn't exactly hug him; he put his arms around Eddie's upper arms the way a football player would grab a tackling dummy.

"Yes," he said, although he could barely talk through his smile. "What are we going to do?"

"You leave that to me," Eddie said confidently. "Now, why don't you pack us some weed so we can get today going?" He smiled and nodded toward the pencil case that William was still holding.

"I will," he confirmed, "but I only have a little bit. Do you think you could introduce me to your new guy?" The timing wasn't exactly coincidental; they were both parts of the same chain reaction of events, but the boys had lost (abandoned) one marijuana dealer for another.

That day, when Phillip snubbed Eddie and his public school friends, Pete introduced Eddie to his dealer. His name was Benjamin, but everyone called him Bentley. He lived in a neighborhood near Grissom High School and serviced about a third of the school's marijuana smokers.

"Yeah," Eddie said. "I'll text him, and we can walk over to his place."

When they left William's, the sun was just starting its slow descent. For now, however, it was still light out, and the boys were ready for an adventure, even if that adventure was just going to buy some weed.

When they reached the front of William's neighborhood, Eddie's phone produced two clear chimes. He checked his messages and saw that Bentley was home and ready for them to come over. They walked the rest of the way without talking much, both smiling.

At times, Eddie mumble-hummed one of their favorite songs. Then he switched to School's Out by Alice Cooper. He only knew the line from the chorus, but it fit the moment, and it hadn't gotten old by the time they approached Bentley's house. When they were a few houses down, Eddie texted him that they were almost there. When they reached the driveway, Bentley was in the doorway, holding back two lively pit bulls by their collars.

"They're sweet," he guaranteed as he welcomed the boys into his home. "Don't worry."

"Hey, Bentley. What's going on?" Eddie asked.

"Not much. Done with school 'til the fall, so everything is alright," Bentley said jovially. "Who's your friend?"

"This is William," Eddie said, then, feeling like he needed to vouch for him, added, "He's a good guy. I've known him forever." He felt a creep of warmth on his cheekbones.

"How come I've never seen you around?" Bentley asked. He wasn't interrogating, more like making small talk, it felt like.

"I go to Woolstead," William explained. He hoped this would not elicit a negative reaction. He was used to people having a misconception about those he went to school with, but when he thought about it, he wasn't entirely sure they were misconceptions when it came to most of his classmates.

"Ok. Ok," Bentley nodded. "I know some Woolstead folks. You don't look like you have a stick up your butt." He felt comfortable enough to make a joke, and it landed. Eddie and William were both laughing. Just to confirm the light mood, William played into it.

"I do," he joked. "Don't worry." Bentley let go of the dog's collars, and they both ran to Eddie, one batting at him with its front paw. He approached William with his right hand extended.

"I'm Bentley," he said, and William shook his hand with vigor.

"Nice to meet you," William said.

"So what can I do for you boys this fine afternoon?" Bentley asked.

"Hoping to get some weed," Eddie said, although Bentley already knew this from their brief texting conversation.

"Fifty dollars worth," William chimed in. "If that's OK."

"A-ok with me," Bentley smiled. "Let's go to my office." He led the way, and when he said office, he meant bedroom. The three boys entered the room, and Bentley attempted to close the door behind them. He got it most of the way closed before the head of a pit bull appeared through the doorway, preventing him from pushing it any farther. "C'mon," he beckoned as he opened the door again to let the dogs follow. The room was small and generally tidy but certainly lived in. Each item bore the mark of familiarity, creating an ambiance that reflected a balance between order and the comfort of personal space. The bed was made, but it looked like Bentley had taken a nap on the bedspread since this morning. The little desk had books and papers scattered over it despite the fact that school was done for the year. Bentley sat at the desk and gestured to the bed.

"Make yourselves at home," he said. He handed William a half-smoked bong and a lighter. "A sample of what you're buying."

"It's ok to smoke in here?" William confirmed.

"Of course," Bentley confirmed. "Have at it." William took a larger puff than he had intended. He hadn't smoked many bongs, and he misjudged how much smoke had accumulated in the bottom. The smoke rushed into his lungs and then back out through his nose and mouth. He coughed twice but quickly regained his composure, though his eyes were now glazed over.

"Good stuff," he said as he handed the bong to Eddie. There was nothing left to smoke, so Eddie put it on the floor between his feet while the other two exchanged goods. "Really good." Bentley opened his desk drawer and retrieved a large bag of marijuana and a small scale. He put the scale on the desk where everyone could see him weigh out the proper amount. This is something Eddie and William had never seen Phillip do.

After learning he ripped Eddie off, they assumed he had been giving bad deals for years. This was a new experience with a seemingly standup person. He put the marijuana into a baggie and handed it to William, who promptly passed back fifty dollars.

"Can I repack that?" William asked, pointing to the bong.

"Of course," Bentley said with a grin. "I'll throw some in too." He emptied the ashes from the bong and handed it to William, who began crumbling weed. Bentley did the same, and less than a minute later, they were ready to smoke. William held out the bong as if to ask who wanted it.

"Odds or evens," Bentley said as he held out a fist. Eddie and William looked at each other, then at Bentley, confused. They had never heard of this game. Bentley explained quickly, and the other two held out their fists. On the count of three, each would hold out one or two fingers. The person who didn't match the other two won and would smoke first. It was not as elaborate as it sounded once the boys understood how to play.

Bend or Break

"One. Two. Three!" Bentley called out. He and William held out two fingers while Eddie held out one. This was simple enough and a fun little game that Eddie would be sure to remember. Within minutes, all three had smoked the bong and were feeling the effects. Eddie, still sitting on the bed, now had a dog in his lap. He and William were exchanging glances and smiling. Bentley picked up on a connection between them.

"Can I ask you something?" he said, but this was just an introduction. He was not shy about asking the real question without waiting for an answer to his rhetorical one. "Are y'all together?" William and Eddie looked at one another and didn't know how to respond.

"We're not together-together," William said, hoping that would explain things.

"But we're not not-together," Eddie added, which both helped explain and added to the confusion. All three boys laughed.

"That works," Bentley said casually. "Doesn't make any difference to me." This was Eddie's first experience not being completely straight with anyone besides William, who only just heard the news recently. It felt good to be in the open. It felt good not to feel judged by anyone.

Saturday came and found both Eddie and William apprehensive about their date. In reality, they both wanted to spend the day together, but Eddie was working, and they had agreed not to meet until six o'clock. The anticipation lingered, heightening the sense of eagerness as the agreed-upon time approached.

The plan was to go to dinner and watch a movie. While it wasn't Eddie's most original plan, it fit the bill for a first date. He had reservations at a nice but not overly fancy Italian restaurant and tickets to an old film they were playing downtown. Although it was a film Eddie hadn't seen, he knew William was interested in the classics like Citizen Kane and The Sting. He hoped the film they were seeing that night, The Bridge on the River Kwai, was not in black and white. There was something about black-and-white movies that felt like they were in slow motion to Eddie.

William didn't know what to do with his day. He thought about going to see Eddie at the Taco Plaza but then decided that was silly. The anticipation of their date that night paralyzed him. He paced the house for a few hours. He went from his room to the kitchen, where he opened the fridge and closed it again without taking anything out. He went from the kitchen to the lounge, where he mindlessly knocked a pool ball and aimlessly threw a dart. He went back to his room, where he stared into his closet, pretending to decide what to wear that night. He was getting ready to play a video game to kill an hour or so when Leah appeared in his doorway.

"You seem antsy today," she observed. "Anything on your mind?"

"I probably shouldn't tell you," he began. She would have stopped him, but she knew the best news started this way. "Eddie and I are going on a date tonight." She blinked and continued to look at her brother, who smiled and looked like he was going to jump off the bed with excitement.

"I thought you ruined each other for dating," she said.

"Well, I didn't mean dating each other," he said, and she cracked a smile that quickly returned to two parallel lips under questioning eyes.

"Are you going to ruin your friendship?" she asked.

"No," he said without questioning himself. He had been worrying about this on and off since he woke up that morning, but he hadn't posed the question so succinctly to himself. Of course, they weren't going to ruin their friendship. They were only going to get closer, right? Leah came fully into the room and gave him a hug.

"I'm really happy for you," she said into his hair as they embraced briefly. When she stepped back, she nodded to the video game console. "Now fire that up so I can show you how it's done."

"Not a chance," William joked back, "you're terrible."

"Not as terrible as you," she said. He was glad for two reasons. She had distracted him from his anticipation, and she had freed him from his paralysis. He wasn't sure if either was intentional, but he was glad to share this with his older sister at this moment.

Eddie's shift ended, and he went home to shower and change before the big date. He had been preoccupied with work all day and hadn't had time to think about the evening.

Bend or Break

Suddenly, his nerves set in, and a bead of sweat arose at his hairline. They decided to meet at the park for a few reasons. First, it was a good halfway point between their houses. Second, it was fairly close to the restaurant Eddie had chosen. Third and most importantly, neither of them wanted to see the other's parents. They hadn't told them yet, but they knew the awkwardness would be too hard to ignore.

Eddie arrived at the park first, remembering something his father had once said about never arriving to a date late. He walked a few laps around the bench and then needed something else to occupy the time and distract his body. He pulled from his pocket some rolling papers and a small amount of marijuana. He crumbled some of the marijuana into one of the papers and rolled it into a rough cigarette. The tactile process of preparing the joint added a ritualistic element, creating a moment suspended in the convergence of craftsmanship and recreation.

As he was licking the paper to seal it, he heard something behind him.

"Sir!" the voice said authoritatively. First, Eddie flinched and dropped the joint he had just finished rolling.

Then he realized it was William playing a joke on him. They laughed as Eddie bent to pick up the rolled paper. Then he stood as William walked around the bench, and then they hugged.

"Is this weird?" Eddie asked softly, kicking a patch of grass with his toe.

"Yes," William smiled back as he responded, "but weird can be good, too." They smiled and settled in to smoke before they headed to dinner. William took his usual spot, sitting on the bench. Instead of his typical position sitting on the back of the bench with his feet on the seat, Eddie sat next to William, nearly elbow to elbow. He put the joint between his lips and introduced the flame of a lighter. As soon as the joint was lit, he passed it to William, who took a puff.

"I feel so lucky," William said, and Eddie looked at him, confused. "I feel like I'm in second grade, and the popular girl gave me a Valentine's Day card." He nudged Eddie's elbow with his.

"Only instead of the popular girl, you're stuck with me," He smiled, "and instead of a box of hearts made of chalk, you get this." William smiled back and handed him the joint. When it was smoked down to a nub, and the boys were sufficiently stoned, they started the short walk to the restaurant. It was a popular Italian joint, and it was busy on a Saturday night, as far as anything was ever busy in Galvin. They arrived right on time and were shown to their table. They were no strangers to dining out, and the restaurant wasn't exactly fancy, but the boys found themselves feeling out of place. They were sitting across from each other at the round table in the middle of the dining room.

It was noisy, and they had to talk a little bit too loud to hear each other. It felt forced, but neither wanted to say anything. They both felt pressure for things to go perfectly, but as they looked through the menus, they both wished they had gotten some subs or done something more casual. William was thinking about tacos, but he doubted Eddie would want to go to the Taco Plaza for much longer.

The meal commenced a little loudly and a little awkwardly, but the food and company were good. They were both glad when the check came. Eddie insisted on paying.

"I do have a job after all," he reminded William with a smile, and William could tell he took pride in paying, which was awfully cute.

On the way to the theater, they walked slowly because they were early. William wondered if he should hold Eddie's hand. Was that too much, too fast? Would they attract attention as two men holding hands in public? He was sure he was overthinking it. Eddie's thoughts were along the same lines because he made an attempt to take William's hand, but he misjudged as William's hand was swinging, and their hands just sort of brushed. The boys laughed awkwardly.

"Why is this so weird?" William asked, momentarily breaking the tension and bringing both boys to the present.

"I thought you said weird was good," Eddie quoted back. They smiled at this, and William nudged Eddie's shoulder with his.

"What movie are we seeing?" William asked, giving Eddie another opportunity to play a joke.

"Well, I couldn't decide between the new romcom and the new Smurfs movie," he said, knowing William would hate both these options, "so I got us a double feature, and we can see both."

They entered the theater, and Eddie managed to get the tickets without William finding out what the movie was.

"Do you want some popcorn?" Eddie asked, and he cringed. He knew William hated popcorn. "Or some candy," he added quickly.

"Nothing for me," William said without pointing out the obvious.

"I'm going to get some Twizzlers," Eddie said.

About thirty minutes into the movie, William woke up and realized he had missed several scenes and lost the plot. He tried to casually look over at Eddie to see if he was enjoying the film. He could tell immediately that it was not Eddie's favorite movie ever, so he leaned in.

"I fell asleep," he admitted.

"I hate this movie," Eddie countered.

"Let's get out of here," William suggested with a smile. They quietly but quickly rose from their seats and exited the theater. Back in the main corridor, heading towards the lobby, Suddenly, they were back to usual. The tension was gone.

"Why did you pick this movie?" William asked.

"I thought you would like it," Eddie said. "And I hoped you would fall asleep," he added with a smirk.

"Wanna go back to the park?" William asked, and of course, Eddie did. They left the theater in better spirits than they had entered less than an hour before.

"Why did we try to turn this into a big deal?" Eddie asked. He was at least as guilty as William. He had tried to be something different than he normally was, and that was the problem. He and William got along as they were, so changing anything meant risking everything they had built over the years.

"I wanted this evening to be special," William admitted.

"Every time we hang out is special," Eddie dared to admit back. "We should have just done our normal thing."

"I agree. Wanna go on an adventure?"

"As long as we can still consider it a date." Eddie bargained.

"Deal," William conceded with a smile. They were both worried, most of all, that the change in their dynamic would put their friendship in jeopardy, but they were also worried about the way forward. They would either fall back into being friends, abandoning the hopes for anything more, or they would have to find a way to retain all the things that made their friendship unique and translate those into a romantic relationship. No option was easy, but falling back into friendship was the path of least resistance, and it wasn't what either of them wanted.

Eddie walked William home, and they stopped at the front door. They were well-illuminated by the sconces on either side of the entranceway. They smiled, and Eddie hesitated.

"Do you want to come in and hang out for a while?" William asked

"On a first date?" Eddie asked with a smile. "What do you take me for?" The boys laughed until Eddie took William's left hand in his right and turned him so they stood face to face. Then Eddie held both of William's hands, and his face turned serious. "I had a lot of fun tonight."

"Me too," William confirmed and looked down shyly. "See you tomorrow?" he added coyly.

"I'll text you after work," Eddie said, and he paused for a moment as William thought he saw a tinge of pink in Eddie's face. Eddie leaned close and gave William the briefest of pecks on the cheek, then he took a step back and released William's hands. "Good night," Eddie said and scurried down the pathway to the sidewalk without another word.

Chapter Fifteen

The next several days passed relatively routinely. Eddie and William saw a lot of each other when Eddie wasn't working. When he was, William found ways to occupy his time. It was the summer, after all, and his expectations were low. There was no need to start on his summer reading yet; he would almost certainly finish well ahead of the school year. It was the first year his older brother was not coming home from college. He had an internship and got an apartment for the summer. That was a bit of a change, but otherwise, it was a normal summer in the Blake home.

William spent much of his time watching mindless TV shows with Leah (courtroom reality shows were a weakness of theirs) or playing video games by himself. One morning, he found himself in an unusual position. He was out of marijuana, and he didn't have Bentley's phone number yet. He had found Bentley's social media profile and considered messaging him to see if it was alright to come by, but he thought better of it. What if Bentley didn't like to discuss business on social media? What if he had a code word he liked people to use? William wanted to treat the new relationship delicately.

Bentley was a new acquaintance of Eddie's and one he had met through Pete. Now that he wasn't speaking to Pete, Ella, and Brian (besides the long and still awkward shifts together at the Taco Plaza), it would be easy for this relationship to fall through the ice. The last thing William wanted was to lose their new and only dealer because he sent a stupid message. He was sure he was overthinking it. Bentley was a nice guy, but it was better to tread lightly.

After considering his messaging options for Bentley, he decided to message Eddie, who was supposed to be at work. "Come over later," he said and was surprised when he got a message back within a minute. Eddie didn't text at work. He knew it was a strict rule.

"I can come over now!" Eddie wrote back, and William saw he was typing another message. "No work today. Meet at the park in 20?"

William replied with a single heart and went to fetch his shoes. As he opened his bedroom door to leave, his sister was standing there in the hallway. She wasn't waiting for him exactly, and she couldn't have been eavesdropping as there was no audible conversation to overhear.

"Where are you going with such a big smile?" she asked. William hadn't noticed he was grinning like a child at an amusement park.

"Just going to meet with Eddie," he said and suddenly felt sheepish at how giddy he was to meet with Eddie ahead of schedule.

"You two seem to be back on good terms," she said, either ignoring or not observing his embarrassment. He wanted to think she hadn't observed it, but he knew that was more wish than reality.

"We…" he started and didn't know how to sum up what had happened in a single passing comment, "patched things up," William continued and hoped this would be enough of an explanation.

"And you haven't seen Matt or Jessica lately," she added, now clearly ignoring his beet-red cheeks. "Not over here, at least."

"How are things with you and Danny?" he asked, trying to change the subject.

"Better than ever," she briefly answered her little brother's question before getting back to the topic at hand. "Have you talked to Matt since he tried to apologize?"

"I'm done with him," William said decisively. "I hope I never see him again."

"Well, you're going to see him again." she declared. William was confused. What was she trying to force? "In school, at parties, around town. You can't go the next two years without seeing him at all."

"I can try," William asserted.

"You know the best way to stop a rumor," she went on, "is to show everyone there is nothing to talk about." William opened his mouth to respond, but she cut him off. "Easier said than done," she added, "but what in life is supposed to be easy?" He opened his mouth again, but once again, she spoke first. "Go on. Eddie's waiting."

This conversation really stuck with William. He was shaken and thought about what Leah said the whole walk to the park. He couldn't take his mind off her words. What did she mean the best way to stop a rumor is to show everyone there is nothing to talk about? What did that even mean? He was frustrated. What good was cryptic advice?

He arrived at the park before Eddie, and his thoughts were racing. *I should have told him I needed to pick up weed. What if he's late because he went by Bentley's? What did Leah mean about stopping a rumor?* What was she trying to tell him? Had she heard something new about him and Matt? Were there rumors about him and Eddie? Of course, there were; there had been rumors about the two of them since eighth grade. When Eddie touched his shoulder, he jumped off the bench, spun around, and grabbed Eddie's hand. The spontaneous reaction encapsulated William's mindset but quickly subsided to palpable excitement.

"Whoa!" Eddie said, "I didn't mean to scare you." The truth was that William's reaction had startled him, and now they were standing on either side of the bench, both wide-eyed and slack-jawed, Eddie's limp hand in William's.

"Sorry," William said, releasing his grip on Eddie. "I was deep in thought."

"About what?"

"I'll tell you about it, but can we text Bentley first?" William asked.

"Yeah, definitely," Eddie said. "I'll text him now, and then we can smoke while we wait for him to respond." He pulled out his pipe and bag of marijuana and handed it to William to pack up. Then, he retrieved his phone and texted Bentley. "I'll ask him if I can give you his number when we see him," Eddie added.

William crumbled some of the dried herb into the bowl of the pipe and tried to hand it back to Eddie. It was Eddie's weed, and he didn't want to be greedy or presumptuous. Eddie smiled and waved him off, telling him to go ahead and smoke while he sent his text message to Bentley. William smiled back and momentarily forgot about his sister's strange advice.

Thirty minutes later, the boys were sufficiently stoned and were walking to Bentley's. He had texted Eddie back to come by anytime until one o'clock. It was barely eleven, so there was plenty of time, but William and Eddie wanted to get the business over with. They had no plans for the day except to waste it together. When they knocked on the door, Bentley didn't hold the dogs back. He opened it wide and let the excited pit bulls run out to dance on the front porch and knock William and Eddie around with their considerable mass.

"You're old friends by now," Bentley joked. "I think they like you more than they like me."

"No way," Eddie consoled through a grin and rubbed the ears of the larger dog. "We just smell new and exciting. Don't we, girl?" saying the last few words to his four-legged companion.

Inside, business was conducted quickly.

"Can I pack us all up a little," William asked. He'd smoked with Eddie and Bentley the last time they were over for Eddie to buy some, so he thought it the polite thing to do. He was right, and he couldn't believe how easy Bentley was to get along with. Maybe they could even hang out with him outside the buyer-dealer relationship.

"Be my guest!" Bentley agreed. It was likely that none of the three of them needed to smoke anymore, but it was social and fun and something to do to pass the time. William opened his new baggie of greens, which was weighed out in front of him, and put some into the bong on the table between them. He handed Bentley the packed water pipe and checked his pockets for a lighter.

"I got one," Bentley said and pulled a blue Bic lighter from his back pocket. He took a big hit of the weed and passed the bong to Eddie on his left, who took his cue to do the same. As Eddie smoked, Bentley put his arms out as though they were great wings. He began to slowly flap them as if they really were wings. He stood up from his seat in perfect timing, so it looked like his arm flapping had lifted him up through levitation. He rolled his head on his neck and made a wild face before announcing, "Dragon!" and exhaling the smoke from his lungs in a great cloud. Eddie and William laughed at this. Bentley coughed a few times and joined the others in laughter. "What are you guys doing tonight?" he asked. Eddie and William looked at each other, surprised, not knowing how to respond right away. Bentley continued, "I'm having a few people over. Nothing crazy, but you should definitely come by. It will be fun."

"Thanks," Eddie said instinctively. Then, he thought through the entire situation. "Are Pete and Ella going to be there?" He felt foolish asking. It was like someone had given him a birthday cake, and he had said sorry, I don't like chocolate. It seemed ungrateful, but he didn't want to run into his brief but former friends.

"Naa," Bentley brayed. "They're just customers. We don't hang out like that." Then he added quickly, "Not that I have anything bad to say about them."

Everyone laughed, and then Eddie and William realized Bentley was waiting for a response. Eddie wanted to make an excuse so he could consult William. Each of their last party-going experiences had ended badly, but this seemed innocent enough. They would have each other, and they could leave whenever they wanted. It seemed low risk when Eddie thought more about it.

"We'll be here," Eddie said. William gave him a nervous smile and nudged his shoulder.

"Not that it's any of my business either," Bentley went on, "but it's a safe space, too." William and Eddie did not immediately know what he meant, so he explained further. "My friends Shauna and Lissa will be there. They're girlfriends." Then, making sure his point was completely driven home, "You know, lesbians." he dragged out the last word into all its component syllables.

"Oh," William said. He didn't know what to say, but he wanted to say something. They all laughed again.

"Yeah. We're all cool here," Bentley reiterated. "Come by around nine. BYOB."

Four hours later, Eddie was waking up and feeling groggy. He blinked his eyes against the sunlight sneaking between the slats of the blinds on the windows. He felt stiff and tried to remember where he was. The disoriented awakening hinted at the hazy aftermath of a deep, restful slumber.

The last thing he could remember was that he and William had gone back to William's house to prepare for the party later. His ribs ached on one side like he was lying on a stone. They had decided to watch a movie and relax before asking Leah to buy them some beer, but he couldn't remember anything after that. He took a deep breath, as deep as he could with his aching ribs, and rolled over, away from the light, to find himself face to face with William. They must have fallen asleep during the movie because William's eyes were closed, and he was breathing softly.

Here, Eddie found himself in William's arms, in William's bed. The aching in Eddie's ribs was from William's arm, which he had been lying on. The pain immediately subsided, and suddenly, Eddie was comfortable and couldn't think of anywhere in the world he would rather be. A wave of tranquility washed over him, the comfort of the moment eclipsing any lingering discomfort.

He rolled back over to look at the window and tried to determine what time it was when he heard William begin to breathe faster and shallower. He was awake.

"Sorry I woke you up," Eddie whispered, rolling back over so they were face to face once more. This is it, he thought. This is love. He remembered a cheesy song his dad used to play and sing along to when he had an extra beer after dinner. "Heaven Can Wait" was what he thought the song was called, and now he understood. Well, he didn't understand his father's off-key rendition, but he got the meaning of the song for the first time in his life. He couldn't imagine being any happier than there in William's arms, the sun slowly descending behind the trees to cast a shadow over them like a blanket. Eddie breathed deeply and tried with all his willpower not to tremble as he inhaled. He was glad he succeeded. William closed his eyes and slowly rolled toward Eddie, who saw that he was puckering his lips. Eddie closed his eyes and felt the pressure of William's soft lips press against his. It was a brief, closed-mouth kiss, but it fit the moment perfectly. Their lips parted, and they both opened their eyes.

"Will you be my boyfriend?" Eddie whispered still. The words came out almost without thinking of them. For a moment, he wondered if he meant them. He wondered if it was a mistake, something he would wish he could take back, but he knew he never could.

"Yes," William whispered back. They smiled and kissed each other again on the lips. "Can I ask you something kind of big?"

"Of course," Eddie responded. "What is it?"

"I want to tell my sister," William said. He wasn't sure why, but he knew he needed to tell someone.

"You know," Eddie said slowly, "I get the impression she already knows. The other day, she came by and talked to me and said something about how you and I couldn't date any girls because we were best friends. Something like that."

Bend or Break

"So is it ok if I tell her?" William wanted to make sure he got a clear answer to his question and didn't make any assumptions that would get him in trouble later.

"It's ok." They both smiled.

"Then I have to ask you one more thing," William said.

"Something else?" Eddie asked with a sarcastic eye roll. "Boyfriends for two minutes, and you're already so needy."

"Can you please get off my arm?" William said with a groan. "I can't feel my hand." They both laughed, and Eddie sat up, relieving the pressure from William's arm. Eddie felt none of the stiffness or pain in his ribs from earlier. He was reinvigorated.

On the walk to Bentley's party, William and Eddie were all smiles. It was so silly when they thought about it. Nothing had really changed. They were calling it a date when they hung out, but they did exactly what they would have done anyway. Now they were calling each other boyfriend, but they were still just hanging out as normal. Only it wasn't normal. It was magical. It was like the day they had met, the day Eddie had helped William after his nose bled from a collision with a red rubber ball. Things between them simply felt special. Neither could think of a better word to describe it. Eddie staggered a few steps toward William and bumped into his shoulder.

"Hey, boyfriend," he said innocently. He tried to hide his smile, but his eyes were reduced to tiny slits that showed how ecstatic he was. With no attempts to conceal his, William responded with a smile of his own.

"Hi, boyfriend," he said back quaintly.

"Ok. That's enough being cute," Eddie jokingly commanded. "We're almost at Bentley's. Let's put on a straight face." The boys stopped where they were and turned toward each other, both on the verge of breaking out laughing. Both said simultaneously, "No pun intended," and as they began cracking up, "Jinx!" Eddie had made an unintentional joke about putting on a straight face. It was a slip of the tongue. This, if possible, brought the two even closer together, and it was just when they needed it. They were both worried and thinking about their party misadventures from the spring. This couldn't be any different, though. First, they were there to look out for each other. If something went wrong, there was no way either of them was going to abandon the other. The unavowed pact of solidarity solidified their bond, creating a foundation of unspoken, mutual support and unwavering commitment.

Second, Bentley had described this as a safe space. Whatever that meant, he was trying to ease their minds. Maybe he had heard about what happened to William and Matt, but they doubted it. They just thought Bentley was being genuine and welcoming. They would soon find out exactly what he meant.

Eddie knocked on the door tentatively. He could hear music coming from inside, but it wasn't thunderously loud. The subdued soundscape hinted at a gathering with a more relaxed atmosphere, providing a subtle preview of the scene awaiting him on the other side.

A moment later, Bentley opened the door, but he was hardly recognizable. His face was covered in the most glamorous makeup William and Eddie had ever seen. There was glitter and rhinestones around his eyes and perfectly faded blush on his cheekbones. He wore a one-piece outfit that looked like it could have come from a nineteen-seventies disco club. The flamboyant ensemble reflected a vibrant fusion of vintage glam and modern flair, capturing attention with its eclectic charm. It was a single, one-piece white jumper with wide-bottomed pant legs and a shooting star embroidered on the chest. Eddie thought Bentley looked like Elton John with a darker complexion, although Eddie wasn't sure he was picturing Elton John correctly.

"Come on in!" he said convivially. "You know me as Bently, but now you can get to know me as Barbie."

"Black Barbie!" someone shouted from behind him. Everyone was laughing, and Eddie and William couldn't tell who had said it. Judging by Bently's (Barbie's) reaction, he wasn't upset about it.

"This is Eddie," Bentley said, getting back to pleasantries and pointing to Eddie, "and this is William." Then he started pointing around the room. "That's Josh. The lezzie's in the corner are Shauna and Lissa. That's Erin and Kwon. Enough… you'll get to know everyone. Come on in." It was certainly the warmest greeting Eddie and William had received from a gathering of peers. If all parties started this way, they might not have been so shy to go out. They would need some time to learn names, but everyone seemed friendly. William took two beers from the case they brought in his leather bag. He handed one to Eddie, and they drank heartily.

"Put those in the fridge and come join the game," someone said. William was half sure it was either Shauna or Lissa, but he wasn't sure which was which or if he was even remembering their names right.

"Let me," Bentley-Barbie said. He took the case of beer, handed William two more with a wink that said, "You'll be needing these," and disappeared into the kitchen with the rest.

"What are we playing?" Eddie asked, hoping it was some game he knew.

"Categories," Someone responded. Kwon, Eddie thought. "It was about to be my turn."

"Was not!" Erin argued. "You just went. It's my turn next."

"Ok. Ok," Kwon said. "Don't get your panties in a bunch." Eddie and William had never been to a party like this. They had never been among a group like this. They didn't know there were people like this in Galvin or even Staunton. These people were proud of who they were.

Some were straight, some were gay, some were bi, queer, and other descriptors on the spectrum of sexuality. No one was hiding or pretending. No one was forced or pressured to be here. It would be a stretch to say that William and Eddie felt comfortable in the group because they had only just arrived. They were still wary of parties and groups and crowds, but they didn't feel uncomfortable, and that was a start. By the time they learned everyone's names, they would all be laughing like old friends. The gradual easing of reservations set the stage for a shared camaraderie, creating a space where familiarity and laughter could bloom.

"So the game is easy," Erin continued. "I'll pick a category, and we go around the circle naming things in the category. If you hesitate, you drink. If you repeat something, you drink. If you say a wrong answer, you drink."

"Got it," Eddie smiled, "I drink." Bentley-Barbie returned from the kitchen with a few beers for Shauna and Lissa and one for himself. He sat on the floor so his guests could have the seats around the coffee table.

Bend or Break

"The category is," Erin said and hesitated for suspense, "Items in the fridge." At this, some of the teens groaned and rolled their eyes. Some smiled. Erin began, "Milk."

"Eggs," Kwon said, sitting to her left. Beside him was Bentley-Barbie on the floor, who chimed in next.

"Beer," he shouted and added, "and can I get an Amen?" to which most of the room shouted "Amen" back. Eddie and William were next, and the game was easy so far.

"Pickles," Eddie said and turned to William to see what he would come up with.

"Ketchup," William said, and this caused an unexpected uproar. As it turned out, after several minutes of debating and voting, the majority of the room did not keep their ketchup in the refrigerator. William protested but sipped his beer to keep the peace.

After the game, the partiers, if you could call the small group a party, mingled and sort of split into groups of two or three. Kwon, Erin, and Bentley-Barbie were huddled in the kitchen, gossiping about some people Eddie and William had never heard of. It could have been they were talking about celebrities or people they knew from school, but the discussion was heated. Josh and someone else went outside to smoke a cigarette. William and Eddie were in the living room with Lissa and Shauna. Lissa had dark, sleek hair that went halfway down her back. She had smooth, olive skin and a small, soft nose. Her lips were barely visible lines on her otherwise fair face. Shauna wasn't heavy, but she was not slender like Lissa. She had short, curly hair that went where it wanted. Her skin had an oily sheen. She wore a black shirt with a rainbow on it. Shauna's unique features and distinctive style painted a vivid picture, celebrating individuality with a touch of rebellious charm.

The words *I'm out* were written over the rainbow on her shirt, and the words *of my mind* were in smaller print below the rainbow. She and Lissa said, "Cheers!" then they clanked their beers together, tapped the beer cans on the table, and kissed each other before taking a big gulp.

"Are you two a couple?" Lissa asked William and Eddie.

"We're…" William started, and he looked from the young woman to Eddie, not knowing the end of his own sentence. He didn't know what Eddie would want him to say. He had asked if they could come out to Leah, but this was coming out to a much wider group.

"We're dating," Eddie finished with a big smile. Lissa and Shauna looked at each other hopelessly.

"Newlyweds," they said in unison and rolled their eyes.

"What does that mean?" Eddie wanted to know

"You're so cute and totally in love with each other," Shauna started to explain.

"Don't worry," Lissa chimed in, "It'll wear off."

"I don't know," William found his voice and stuck up for his best friend and new boyfriend. "We've known each other for a long time."

"Yeah," Eddie agreed. "We've been best friends since second grade."

"Aha!" Lissa interjected. "Best friends, sure, but how long have you been boyfriends?" Everyone was smiling, and the questioning was friendly in nature.

"Well, technically," William began, and everyone laughed, including him and Eddie. "Technically," he went on through the laughter. "We just made it official today, but really, it's been a few weeks." Lissa made a shrill squeak and closed her eyes.

"They are so cute," said Lissa. "We're officially adopting you two as our gaybies." She didn't have to explain this term. William rolled his eyes at the idea, but he also felt the spark of a connection forming a new friendship.

"Don't overwhelm them, Lissa!" Shauna said. "You can see they're new to all this." Then, turning to Eddie, "It's easier to tell a stranger, isn't it?"

"Yes," Eddie said with a huge cartoonish sigh. "Why is that?"

"We don't know you," Shauna explained. "We don't have any preconceived notions of who you are or who you aren't."

"Also, we're new," Lissa added. "If you tell us you're gay and we don't like you, it's not like you've lost a friend. It's low risk."

"That makes sense," Eddie said, and it really did. It explained why it had been so hard to tell his best friend in the world but easy to tell a stranger. He was afraid that when he told William, something would change between them. Admittedly, things had changed between them, but that's not what he was nervous about. It was a paradox if he'd ever heard one, but Lissa and Shauna obviously had gone through the same thing.

"Wanna go out back and smoke?" Shauna asked. "I assume if you know Barbie, then you must smoke weed." William and Eddie both had flashbacks to their previous parties, where they had each gone to the backyard to smoke weed with someone they trusted. They were let down in different ways, but these people in front of them now were not the people who had hurt them. William remembered a quote he had learned in drama class years earlier. He couldn't remember the writer, but it gave him a little comfort. Whoever wrote it, *the scalded dog fears cold water* was ringing in his head. He had been scalded. He and Eddie both had in the past and here they were, mingling with the cold water that was Shauna and Lissa. Why should they fear their new friends?

"Let's go!" William said with a smile, and all four teens stood. Shauna led them to the back door through the kitchen, where Kwon and Erin were drinking with Bentley.

"We're going out back to smoke some greens," Lissa told the group congregated in the kitchen.

"Well, well," Kwon said with a sarcastic attitude. "Don't invite us, why don't you."

"We'll meet you out there, actually," Bentley said. "I'll roll a blunt, and we'll get the party going."

"I've never smoked a blunt," William half-admitted, half-announced. He didn't mean to say it out loud.

"Oh, it's on, preppy boy," Bentley said, more in the Barbie persona this time. Shauna and Lissa led William and Eddie out back and left the three others in the kitchen to get to work rolling the blunt.

"What did he mean by 'preppy boy?'" Shauna asked as they went out back and headed for the cement table positioned on the corner of the paved brick patio.

"I'm guessing it's because I go to Woolstead," William said, hoping this would not garner judgment. He was still guarded, but he was getting more comfortable by the minute.

"Oh, we're in the presence of royalty," Lissa said, dramatically rolling the R in royalty and curtseying with an imaginary skirt.

"Eddie used to go there too," William tried to deflect, but it did no good. Eddie would have stood up for him if he thought William was in distress, but he could tell he was having a good time.

"Don't lump me in with that crowd," he joked. "I've been at Grissom long enough to undo anything I learned there." Everyone laughed, and then the group broke into two conversations. Lissa was talking to Eddie about music, while Shauna was eager to learn more about William.

"So who's your favorite singer?" Lissa asked Eddie as they waited for the guys inside to finish rolling the blunt and join them at the cement table.

"Tough question," Eddie said to buy himself a minute to think. It was a loaded question. Everyone has his own taste in music, and everyone judges others' tastes. "Um, I've been listening to a lot of Coldplay lately." He cringed as he said it in case she deemed it an unacceptable response.

"We can work with that," she said without a gram of judgment. "I saw them in the city last summer."

"No way!" Eddie said, amazed. "I'd love to see them, but I've only been to one concert."

"Stick with me," Lissa went on. "Before you know it, you'll be in a hot tub with them backstage." She and Eddie laughed. Meanwhile, Shauna was talking to William, and the four of them together was the most natural thing in the world.

"So what's it like at Woolsteed?" She asked. William wasn't sure if she mispronounced the name intentionally or not, but it sounded like a funny nickname. William smiled but knew better than to laugh in case it was a mistake. He really liked his new acquaintances so far, and the last thing he wanted was to embarrass anyone.

"I've always gone there, so I don't have anything to compare it to," he said honestly.

"Fair enough," she said, and he could tell she wanted some details. He wanted to share without seeming like he was bragging.

"They're planning a trip to Spain," he added, probably sounding too eager. "But I'm not going."

"Why not?"

"I take French, and my parents say it would be a waste," he explained. By now, Bentley, Kwon, and Erin were coming through the back door from the kitchen to the patio. Bentley held the blunt to his lips and moved his fingers like he was pushing the valves of a tiny trumpet. He made a sound like he was announcing the entrance of a king.

"Duhn duhn-duhn-duhn-duhn duhn-DUHN," he trumpeted, and everyone applauded. Eddie and William joined in the clapping. Bentley lit the blunt carefully and handed it to William. A flash of fear ran through him. Suddenly, he imagined himself lighting his hair on fire, dropping the blunt, and watching it burn into a pile of ash while his new friends looked on. He snapped back to reality and accepted the blunt carefully. He took a puff and started coughing.

"I've never smoked a blunt before," he said again while trying to catch his breath.

"He's used to smoking with the queen," Bentley joked. "And she only smokes from the finest crystal." He waved his pinky as he said this like he was drinking tea. William knew this was all in fun and wasn't insulted by his jokes.

"It's actually fine China," he jokingly corrected as he regained his composure.

Two and a half hours later, Eddie and William were back at William's house in their beds. William was in his pajamas and barely disturbed the blankets while Eddie slept in his undershirt and a pair of lounge pants William had lent him. His sheets, as always, were a mess. They were both fatigued from a night of socializing as much as from the intoxication of alcohol and weed.

"Tonight was perfect," Eddie said. He was in the pullout bed with his back turned toward William.

"Yes, it was perfect," William agreed, and they both drifted off to sleep without another word.

Chapter Sixteen

Two weeks had passed, and summer was in full swing. Eddie and William were as inseparable as ever, with Eddie spending most nights sleeping at William's house. Even on days when he worked a late shift, he would only go home long enough to shower and change his clothes. Now, the sleepers were as different as they were the same. The days and evenings were much as they had always been. They would go on adventures, they would smoke marijuana in the park, and they would narrowly avoid getting into trouble all the while. The familiar rhythm of their shared experiences painted a tapestry of companionship, where each escapade contributed to the rich fabric of their bond. They played pranks on unsuspecting convenience store clerks. Only now, when they left the store in a fit of laughter, they were always able to restrain the giggles long enough for a kiss.

Sometimes, their lips would softly touch and then release almost as soon as they met. Sometimes, they lingered longer, and exploratory tongues would meet for a quick wrestle.

When evenings set in, they made up the beds as usual, but Eddie no longer slept in the pull-out. This was a ruse for the sake of William's parents. Although the boys were sure his parents knew they were a couple, they didn't exactly want them to know they were sleeping in the same bed. Nothing had happened beyond kissing and cuddling, but parents' imaginations don't typically sway toward innocent assumptions. The gap between innocent affection and parental concerns highlighted the nuanced challenges of navigating the complexities of relationships, where perceptions often diverged from the reality of shared moments. So the pull-out bed was pulled out, and a blanket was haphazardly thrown over it, but it remained cold every night.

William was sure his parents knew because he was sure Leah had told them. This was fine with him, as it saved him the trouble. Leah herself found out one day when she walked in on William and Eddie watching a movie in William's bed, although to say she found out would be a slight stretch. It would be more accurate to say she confirmed what she already knew. It was just after nine o'clock, and they were watching a sequel that Eddie insisted was better than the original. William was lying on his back as Eddie lay on his side, nestled against him. William's left arm was around Eddie's shoulder, and Eddie's left arm was on William's sternum, feeling his rhythmic heartbeat. Suddenly, the door swung open. The boys lurched with surprise but didn't jump away from each other as they were neither hiding anything nor feeling guilty for what they were doing.

"So you're official now?" she asked with little interest. She may as well have been asking if it was still raining or not.

"Yes," William said flatly as he and Eddie smiled. Eddie tugged a crease of William's shirt and half hid his face, still grinning uncontrollably and now burning a little.

"Finally," She said as she rolled her eyes, closed the door, and continued with whatever she was doing before she interrupted. As the door clicked, the boys exploded with laughter until the mattress was moving with them, wobbling its springs in time with their amusement.

Not only were Eddie and William spending most of their time together again, but they were also seeing a lot of Lissa and Shauna since they met at Bentley's party. The four of them would go to the city or down the river. They hung out at the park and went to the movies. For Eddie and William, who were not used to larger social circles, it was somehow casual and easy. It was how they always imagined a friendship could be, but something they had only found in each other until now. The newfound ease within a larger social context echoed the profound connection they had initially discovered, expanding their shared vision of meaningful connections beyond their intimate bond.

As their relationship progressed past friendship into something more, they found it was possible to forge a new friendship. Perhaps it was not exactly the same as their friendship had been, but Shauna and Lissa were becoming good friends, and the four were forming something of a crew. William tried not to get his hopes up. He reminded himself that they would all be in college in a few years, so they were on borrowed time anyway. No matter how he framed it, he couldn't think of a time he was happier. He had all the simple desires he could fathom. He had love. It was an emotion that would change over time, and being in love at twenty years old might not feel like it did at fifteen, but he knew it felt right. He had friends who cared about him, people who were interested in his happiness and wanted to hear about the insignificant details of his life. All their lives were generally typical, but as friends, they took the time to care about the mundane minutiae.

This Friday, Eddie was not working, so Shauna insisted they go on a group date. It was the first official date that William and Eddie had gone on since their initial attempt. They lay in bed, William on his back and Eddie nestled beside him. William was mindlessly stroking Eddie's upper arm with his hand while Eddie looked up and twirled a lock of William's hair. They were listening to music, although neither were paying any attention. They were lost in thought, the way that only happens when you are happy and in love.

"Are you ready for tomorrow?" William asked, referring to the date.

"What is there to get ready for?" Eddie asked, letting go of the twisted bit of William's hair and resting his hand on his chest.

"I just mean… are you ready?" William said back and realized that he hadn't clarified anything. "Last time. I don't know."

"I know what you mean," Eddie helped him find the right words. "We put too much pressure on ourselves to make it something more than it was."

"Right."

"But tomorrow will be easy," Eddie went on. "We'll be with Lissa and Shauna, and they are never serious." This was true and made William smile. The two of them had a childlike playfulness that made it hard to imagine an awkward moment.

"True," William said. He seemed less nervous now.

"And we learned our lesson last time," Eddie continued. "Just because we're calling it a date doesn't mean it has to be formal or anything." William felt reassured. He gave Eddie's shoulder a squeeze and looked into the endless sky of his grey eyes. Eddie closed those eyes and pressed his lips against William's.

They spent the next day together in their usual mischief until it was time to prepare for the double date. The plan was to meet at the Maritime Museum at three thirty and then go to dinner afterward. They hadn't chosen where they would eat yet, but they decided it would be somewhere casual. It was time for Eddie to head home to get ready.

"See you at the museum?" Eddie asked as he prepared to leave William's house and walk home. William was beginning to tense up. "Or we can meet at the park at three," Eddie added. At this, William's shoulders loosened, and his face relaxed.

"Thanks," he said. They hugged, and Eddie left. William went back to his bedroom to decide what to wear. He showered, ran his fingers through his wet hair, now even longer during the summer months, and slowly got dressed. He tried not to overthink what he was wearing and went downstairs. He saw Leah in the kitchen rummaging for a snack.

"How are things with you and Danny?" he asked, but that wasn't really the question on his mind.

"Actually, really good," she said. "Why? How are things with you and Eddie?"

"They're fine," he said sheepishly. It wasn't like William to search for his words or not to say what he meant.

"Well?" she prompted.

"We're going on a double date today," he began, "and last time we went on a date, things felt weird."

"That's because you're thinking of it as a date," she said and bonked him lightly on his head with a spoon she had just pulled from the drawer.

"What do you mean?"

"How many hours have you spent with Eddie in your life?" she asked.

"I don't know."

"Like a million," she answered for him, "so why should a few hours today make you nervous?" He cocked his head and raised an eyebrow, asking her to continue. "So it's a date. Who cares? Keep it casual. You were best friends before you were boyfriends." That last piece sunk in, and William found himself more relaxed.

"Did I ever tell you about my first date with Danny?"

"No."

"It was awful. I wore an embarrassing dress like I was a bride's maid, and he brought flowers to the door like we were going to prom."

"So what?"

"So," she explained, "you know what we did on our second date?"

"What?"

"We watched football in our sweatpants." He got her point. "And just remember," she added with a smirk, "if you blow it, you'll lose your boyfriend and your best friend." William let out an audible sigh and stole her spoon from the yogurt she had started eating.

"Give that back!" she shouted, and he pulled the spoon in preparation to fling the yogurt at her. "Don't you dare!" she commanded, although they were both laughing, "or you'll lose a sister, too." They laughed harder, and William finally returned the spoon as he turned to leave and meet Eddie at the park.

He went through to the entrance of the house and tied his shoes. He turned the doorknob and felt ready for the day ahead of him. Then, as he opened the door, the weight of the whole house fell on him. There was Matt standing on the front porch, working up the nerve to ring the bell. William's throat closed up, and his feet felt stuck to the floor. He lost his breath and nearly lost his balance as well.

"I…" Matt began, struggling to get the word out and not immediately finding the next words to follow it. William searched for his breath.

"What are you doing here?" he still felt dizzy and lightheaded. He stepped outside and shut the door.

"I…" Matt said again. "We need to talk."

"We already talked," William found an ounce of confidence as he spoke the words with a frown. "There's nothing to say."

"I'm sorry," Matt said. He seemed genuine as his eyes welled with tears and his cheeks flushed hot red.

"You already said that," William pushed back, "and I still don't accept your apology."

"But I was just scared," Matt said back. "I see that now. There was nothing to be afraid of. You showed me that, Will." William shuttered despite himself.

"Don't call me that!" he snapped.

"I'm sorry," Matt refrained. "I'm not scared anymore." He took a step toward William, whose back was now against the door. He moved closer and looked like he was going for a kiss until William held out his hand and pushed back against Matt's chest. William could feel Matt's heartbeat through his shirt and felt his own pace quicken. Was it because of his newly found strength or the touch of someone he formerly had feelings for? He decided, even in the moment, that it was the former. Any feelings he ever had for Matt had been converted to anger and pity long ago. The emotional metamorphosis marked a definitive shift, transforming the remnants of affection into complex emotions, signaling the closure of a chapter and the emergence of a new emotional landscape.

"Stop," William said, and Matt took a step back. William blinked as he found his words. "I'm glad you've found yourself, and you're not scared anymore," he started, "but don't you realize what you did to me? You humiliated me. I liked you a lot, and you made it seem like we were doing something wrong."

"I know," Matt said as a tear rolled down his cheek and slid along his jawbone toward his chin. "We weren't doing anything wrong," he confirmed.

"I know," William echoed.

"I get it," Matt admitted. "I blew it." His shoulders slumped, and he looked down at the ground between them. "Do you think you could ever forgive me?"

"I can forgive you," William said, "but I can't let you hurt me again. I'm not mad, and maybe in time, we can even be friends again."

"I would like that," Matt said without looking up. A tear fell from his chin and landed on his shoe.

"But for now, I need some space," William said, "and I need you to know that Eddie and I are dating." Matt inhaled sharply like he'd tasted something bitter.

"I understand," he barely said. William took Matt by the shoulders, and Matt looked up. His eyes were red and swollen from the tears, but he managed to smile. "Friends, then?" he asked.

"We'll work on it," William compromised, and for a half second, there was a small glimpse of their old friendship, "but right now, I have to go."

"Right," Matt said with a sniffle as we wiped his nose on his shirt sleeve. They hugged quickly and walked down the driveway in silence. William was thinking how lucky he was that when they got to the street, he would be going one way to the park, and Matt would be going the other way towards his own house. He wasn't sure they would be able to repair their friendship, but he was open to the possibility. He had other friends on his mind. By now, Eddie would be waiting for him at the park.

www.ingramcontent.com/pod-product-compliance
Lightning Source LLC
LaVergne TN
LVHW041755060526
838201LV00046B/1008